FROZEN IN TIME
DI SALLY PARKER
BOOK FOURTEEN

M A COMLEY

For my rock, my beautiful mother, who is now watching over me. Dementia sucks. Remembering all the good times we shared together.

You took a huge chunk of my heart with you. Love you and will miss you, until we're reunited once more.

ACKNOWLEDGMENTS

Special thanks as always go to @studioenp for their superb cover design expertise.

My heartfelt thanks go to my wonderful editor Emmy and my proofreaders Joseph and Barbara for spotting all the lingering nits.

Thank you also to my amazing ARC Group who help to keep me sane during this process.

To Mary, gone, but never forgotten. I hope you found the peace you were searching for my dear friend. I miss you each and every day.

ALSO BY M A COMLEY

Blind Justice (Novella)

Cruel Justice (Book #1)

Mortal Justice (Novella)

Impeding Justice (Book #2)

Final Justice (Book #3)

Foul Justice (Book #4)

Guaranteed Justice (Book #5)

Ultimate Justice (Book #6)

Virtual Justice (Book #7)

Hostile Justice (Book #8)

Tortured Justice (Book #9)

Rough Justice (Book #10)

Dubious Justice (Book #11)

Calculated Justice (Book #12)

Twisted Justice (Book #13)

Justice at Christmas (Short Story)

Prime Justice (Book #14)

Heroic Justice (Book #15)

Shameful Justice (Book #16)

Immoral Justice (Book #17)

Toxic Justice (Book #18)

Overdue Justice (Book #19)

Unfair Justice (a 10,000 word short story)

Irrational Justice (a 10,000 word short story)

Seeking Justice (a 15,000 word novella)

Caring For Justice (a 24,000 word novella)
Savage Justice (a 17,000 word novella)
Justice at Christmas #2 (a 15,000 word novella)
Gone in Seconds (Justice Again series #1)
Ultimate Dilemma (Justice Again series #2)
Shot of Silence (Justice Again series #3)
Taste of Fury (Justice Again series #4)
Crying Shame (Justice Again series #5)
To Die For (DI Sam Cobbs #1)
To Silence Them (DI Sam Cobbs #2)
To Make Them Pay (DI Sam Cobbs #3)
To Prove Fatal (DI Sam Cobbs #4)
To Condemn Them (DI Sam Cobbs #5)
To Punish Them (DI Sam Cobbs #6)
To Entice Them (DI Sam Cobbs #7)
To Control Them (DI Sam Cobbs #8)
To Endanger Lives (DI Sam Cobbs #9)
To Hold Responsible (DI Sam Cobbs #10)
To Catch a Killer (DI Sam Cobbs #11)
To Believe The Truth (DI Sam Cobbs #12)
To Blame Them (DI Sam Cobbs #13)
To Judge Them (DI Sam Cobbs #14)
To Fear Him (DI Sam Cobbs #15)
Forever Watching You (DI Miranda Carr thriller)
Wrong Place (DI Sally Parker thriller #1)
No Hiding Place (DI Sally Parker thriller #2)
Cold Case (DI Sally Parker thriller#3)
Deadly Encounter (DI Sally Parker thriller #4)

Lost Innocence (DI Sally Parker thriller #5)
Goodbye My Precious Child (DI Sally Parker #6)
The Missing Wife (DI Sally Parker #7)
Truth or Dare (DI Sally Parker #8)
Where Did She Go? (DI Sally Parker #9)
Sinner (DI Sally Parker #10)
The Good Die Young (DI Sally Parker #11)
Coping Without You (DI Sally Parker #12)
Could It Be Him (DI Sally Parker #13)
Frozen In Time (DI Sally Parker #14)
Echoes of Silence DI Sally Parker #15)
Web of Deceit (DI Sally Parker Novella)
The Missing Children (DI Kayli Bright #1)
Killer On The Run (DI Kayli Bright #2)
Hidden Agenda (DI Kayli Bright #3)
Murderous Betrayal (Kayli Bright #4)
Dying Breath (Kayli Bright #5)
Taken (DI Kayli Bright #6)
The Hostage Takers (DI Kayli Bright Novella)
No Right to Kill (DI Sara Ramsey #1)
Killer Blow (DI Sara Ramsey #2)
The Dead Can't Speak (DI Sara Ramsey #3)
Deluded (DI Sara Ramsey #4)
The Murder Pact (DI Sara Ramsey #5)
Twisted Revenge (DI Sara Ramsey #6)
The Lies She Told (DI Sara Ramsey #7)
For The Love Of… (DI Sara Ramsey #8)
Run for Your Life (DI Sara Ramsey #9)

Cold Mercy (DI Sara Ramsey #10)

Sign of Evil (DI Sara Ramsey #11)

Indefensible (DI Sara Ramsey #12)

Locked Away (DI Sara Ramsey #13)

I Can See You (DI Sara Ramsey #14)

The Kill List (DI Sara Ramsey #15)

Crossing The Line (DI Sara Ramsey #16)

Time to Kill (DI Sara Ramsey #17)

Deadly Passion (DI Sara Ramsey #18)

Son of the Dead (DI Sara Ramsey#19)

Evil Intent (DI Sara Ramsey #20)

The Games People Play (DI Sara Ramsey #21)

Revenge Streak (DI Sara Ramsey #22)

Seeking Retribution (DI Sara Ramsey #23)

Gone… But Where? (DI Sara Ramsey #24)

Last Man Standing (DI Sara Ramsey #25)

I Know The Truth (A Psychological thriller)

She's Gone (A psychological thriller)

Shattered Lives (A psychological thriller)

Evil In Disguise – a novel based on True events

Deadly Act (Hero series novella)

Torn Apart (Hero series #1)

End Result (Hero series #2)

In Plain Sight (Hero Series #3)

Double Jeopardy (Hero Series #4)

Criminal Actions (Hero Series #5)

Regrets Mean Nothing (Hero series #6)

Prowlers (Di Hero Series #7)

Sole Intention (Intention series #1)

Grave Intention (Intention series #2)

Devious Intention (Intention #3)

Cozy mysteries

Murder at the Wedding

Murder at the Hotel

Murder by the Sea

Death on the Coast

Death By Association

Merry Widow (A Lorne Simpkins short story)

It's A Dog's Life (A Lorne Simpkins short story)

A Time To Heal (A Sweet Romance)

A Time For Change (A Sweet Romance)

High Spirits

The Temptation series (Romantic Suspense/New Adult Novellas)

Past Temptation

Lost Temptation

Clever Deception (co-written by Linda S Prather)

Tragic Deception (co-written by Linda S Prather)

Sinful Deception (co-written by Linda S Prather)

PROLOGUE

How fortunate am I to be accepted by these people?

It was something he'd contemplated for a while now, especially in his new role at the largest secondary school in the Norfolk area. He'd moved to England from Nigeria over five years ago. Had managed to secure a job at a primary school virtually the day after he'd arrived and had been applying for other positions ever since then, in the hope that someone would take a risk on him. He knew he was capable of doing anything and everything he was asked to do, but it wasn't always easy convincing heads of schools of his abilities, despite his impressive qualifications.

That's why he now regarded himself blessed to have settled into his position at St Joseph's. The head, Mrs White, had fortunately taken a real shine to him, and she seemed very eager to help him get established with the children. She'd welcomed him with open arms the day he'd applied for the position. She'd dismissed his shyness once she'd offered him the role at her school. Insisted that she'd seen only good in him and that he needed to feel more confident, otherwise the children were going to eat him alive. He often chuckled when he remembered the conversation which had taken place when Mrs White had personally shown him around the school. She had been an inspiration to him and had believed in him from the first day.

Mrs White continued to push him, sent him on training courses she felt would benefit his future career, enhancing his chances of rising up the ladder quickly. Which was where he was today. Taking his final session on his latest course. He'd reported back to her on day one, told her how much he was enjoying being back in class again. She'd been thrilled to hear the news and wished him good luck.

The course was in Suffolk, not too far from his home in Norfolk. The tutor completed the class and asked the group of teachers for their feedback. Elijah had been enthusiastic in his praise for what he'd learnt over the past week; apparently, far more than the others because they all sat there quietly while he chuntered on, recapping the significant points he'd absorbed from the classes.

The tutor had nodded appreciatively and sent them on their way. The other attendees had rapidly left the room whereas Elijah preferred to take his time, aware that his train wasn't due to depart for another thirty minutes and that it would only take him five to walk to the station.

He got involved in a lengthy conversation with Mr Fisher who seemed as enthusiastic as Elijah was, and the tutor even invited Elijah to walk with him to his vehicle to continue their exchange.

"You're definitely one of the brightest people I've had on my course over the years, Elijah. You could bottle that enthusiasm of yours and sell it down the market on a Saturday, you know, in your spare time."

Elijah laughed. "Thank you, sir, it might be something I consider in the future if Mrs White ever gets fed up with me."

"She won't. I can tell she has a soft spot for you. It's a struggle today to find teachers with as much passion for their role as you have."

"Really? Are you sure? I've always considered teaching as a calling, never really regarded it as a career, if that makes sense?"

"It does and I can tell. Didn't you notice how many questions the others asked in comparison?"

He shrugged. "I guess. I never really thought about it at the time. Once I get started on a subject I'm interested in, I find it very difficult to restrain myself."

"It shows. Don't ever change, Elijah. You're an amazing young man, your parents must be proud of you."

"I think they would be, sir, if they were alive today. Sadly, my father died when I was three, and my mother did her best to raise me until I was sixteen. Then I was sent away to work with a family I didn't know. They were kind to me. I worked ten hours a day, working the land. My mother died when I was seventeen." He tapped his temple. "But up here, that's where I'm blessed. I started reading at a young age; most children only ever played football, hoping to be the next George Weah, the first African to win the FIFA Player of the Year award, but I wasn't really into football back then. I knew from the day I picked up my first book that I wanted to teach."

"And from what I can see, I believe you made a sterling choice, Elijah. Keep up the good work. Here's my number. If ever you need to discuss any of the topics I've covered this week, don't hesitate to get in touch with me. Do you have any plans for the weekend?"

"I'm meeting up with some friends in London, as it is a Bank Holiday."

"Excellent, have a great time unwinding."

"Thank you, I will."

All the way back to London, Elijah stared at the card he'd been given. The kindness of the tutor had truly touched his heart. Not everyone in this country had taken to him since his arrival. Most of the people who knew him treated him kindly, but there were others he'd encountered throughout his five years since moving from Nigeria, who had looked down their noses at him for being black. Racism was rearing its head again in the UK, whether people chose to accept it or not. Depending on what side you were sitting on.

For this reason, Elijah tended to keep his head down, afraid to begin a conversation when he travelled on public transport in case the other passengers took it the wrong way. He hated this part of his life. Struggled to understand why people felt the necessity to be cruel in such circumstances. Was it ignorance? Or intentional? He'd yet to figure that out.

HIS WEEKEND IN LONDON, staying with his friends, turned out to be a great way for him to unwind after his tough week in the classroom.

He left the train and walked the two miles or so home from the station. He didn't have access to a vehicle—well, that wasn't quite true, he'd rescued a rusty bike from a skip he was walking past one day and spent a couple of weekends making it rideable again. He rode that to work every day, which was fine when the weather was decent but not so good in the torrential rain they often experienced. He still felt blessed, having transport, no matter how rusty and inferior it was. That bike was more than he'd had back in Africa, and he absolutely treasured it. One day soon, he hoped to have enough money to save up for a car, a little run-around. He'd been taking driving lessons for the past few months and had passed his test with flying colours. Now all he had to do was save up for a second-hand car, but he knew that would be a long time in his future. The price of running a vehicle lately had gone through the roof.

Elijah sighed at the prospect and placed his key in the front door. The nights were drawing in now. He arrived home at nine and switched on the hall light, except it didn't come on. Cursing under his breath, he went through to the lounge and did the same in there, but still the room remained in darkness. He returned to the hallway and checked the fuse box to find the switch had tripped. That was the key; he turned it back on, and the flat lit up. He took his bag through to the bedroom and left it on the bed to unpack later. For now, he had one thing on his mind, knocking up some supper to battle his hunger pangs. He kicked himself for not stopping off at the corner shop to collect some fresh milk and bread, knowing that he had very little in the cupboards and anything he had in the fridge had gone off.

He went through to the kitchen to see what he could find but, as expected, the cupboards and fridge were lacking, for want of a better word. It was then that he noticed it. A foul smell that he found offensive.

"Oh my goodness, why hadn't I noticed that before?" He continued to search the kitchen to try and locate the source of the putrid odour. It smelt like either the drains were blocked or something had died. The month before, he'd had problems with rodents getting into the flat. He checked the access point, only to find it still boarded up, so he was able to rule that out right away.

Next, he ran the water in the kitchen and flushed the toilet in the bathroom; both appeared to be working well. His flat was on the ground floor. It didn't take long to hunt through the kitchen, lounge and only bedroom, not forgetting the bathroom. But he failed to find out where the foul odour was coming from. The only other possible place was the cellar, however, he didn't have access to that because his landlord kept it padlocked. Apprehension took hold at that point. He'd reluctantly had to query something with his landlord, Collingwood, the month before, when he'd had the rodent issue and he'd been told to get it sorted himself and not to bother Collingwood again. Which had seemed ridiculous to him, but he didn't want to ring the landlord again, thinking the man might get shirty with him and evict him from the flat.

He sat in the lounge and pondered what his next move should be. All the while the stench appeared to be getting worse. Eventually, he rummaged in his briefcase for his mobile. "Hey, Dick, yes, it's me, Elijah. How are you doing, mate?"

"I'm all right, pal. How's it going with you?"

"Umm… not so good. I've got a dreadful smell in the flat, I think it's coming from the cellar, but my landlord keeps it locked. I wondered if you wouldn't mind helping me out."

"Want me to come over and get in there, take a look for you?"

"Would you?"

"Of course. I'll finish off my dinner and come round, how's that? I'll be about thirty minutes."

"I can't thank you enough. See you soon." Elijah ended the call and contemplated if he'd have enough time to get to the shop and back before his builder friend showed up. A couple of minutes of trying to block out the stench made his mind up for him. He ran to the shop and back and arrived home just in time to see Dick pull up in his van. "Hey, great timing, my friend. I appreciate you coming to my rescue."

"Let me get a few tools from the back of the van."

"Sure, you might want to wear a mask as well, honestly, the stench is disgusting."

"Hey, I've spent my life dealing with dodgy drains."

Elijah nodded and smiled. "I still don't think you've smelt anything like this."

"Lead the way, good man, let's take a look at it for you."

Bolt cutters in hand, Dick followed Elijah through the house. "Christ, you weren't wrong. How long has it been like this?"

"I've been away for the week, attending a course. I came home and discovered the switch had tripped. I presume there must have been a power cut while I was away."

"Ah, right. Yes, that's possible, we had a bad storm on Monday or Tuesday. No, it was Monday because the missus was pestering me to do something about it as she was missing out on *Coronation Street*. Unfortunately, there was nothing I could do except ring the supplier. They told me some of the lines had been knocked out in the area and they were doing their best to get the power connected to the thousands of homes in the community that had been affected."

"Ah, right, that explains it. Even though the electricity came back on in the area, it wouldn't here, not until the fuse box had been switched on again."

"Exactly that, mate. Let's see what all the fuss is about down there, eh?" The bolt cutters made light work of the padlock, and it dropped to the floor within seconds.

"I hope I don't get in trouble for doing this," Elijah said, his nerves jangling, his mouth dried up.

"Did you try contacting the landlord?"

"No, I was too scared to after what happened the last time."

"Ah, the rat issue. Yeah, he treated you appallingly over that. I couldn't believe it when you told me. Serves him right. I agree with you, the stench is definitely coming from down here."

"Glad about that, I thought I was going out of my mind

for a second or two." Elijah flicked the switch on the wall at the top of the stairs, but the light didn't come on.

"Don't worry, I've got a powerful torch in the van, I'll fetch it."

Elijah paced the hallway until Dick returned.

His friend led the way down the stairs. "Shit, it's even worse down here."

Dick had supplied Elijah with a mask, but even that failed to stop the smell from permeating.

"What the fuck? Hey, I'd say this is your problem right here. Did you know there was a freezer down here?"

"No, not at all. That does seem strange. Maybe the landlord forgot about it."

Dick raised an eyebrow. "If you insist. If the power was off then whatever is in there has thawed out, which will account for the stench."

"Should I get some black bags? If the food has gone off, the smell is only going to get worse, isn't it?"

"Yeah, might be an idea. Hang on, let's see what we're dealing with first." Dick opened the lid of the large chest freezer and screamed before he instinctively slammed it shut again. "Holy fucking crap!"

"I'm almost afraid to ask what's in there."

Dick ran a shaking hand around his face and over the mask, covering his mouth. "You don't want to know. It explains the damn pong, though. Jesus, your next call should be to the police."

"What? No way. Why?" Elijah plucked up the courage to lift the lid and dropped it when he saw two brown eyes staring back at him. He clutched a hand to his chest; his breathing had become erratic, and acid burnt his throat. He ran to the corner and vomited. "I'm sorry. I've never seen anything like this before. We… I… we… can't leave it here."

"What are you saying? I've told you what to do, call the ruddy police, let them deal with it."

"I can't. I'm an immigrant, they'll deport me."

"What are you telling me? That you're here illegally? Shit!"

"No, not at all. But that won't stop people thinking badly of me, especially the authorities. You have no idea how they treat people like me."

"I'm sorry, I had no idea. I genuinely thought if you had a job and the correct paperwork to live in this country that you'd be safe."

"You'd think so, but there are some coppers who think negatively about people like me. Do I have to remind you of what is going on in the Met Police at the moment?"

Dick raised his hands and shook his head. "Hey, no, you don't. Enough said, pal. What do you propose doing about this then? The body can't stay in there, that isn't going to get rid of the smell."

"We'll have to get rid of it."

"What's with the *we*? I ain't doing nothing dubious like that. No way. I can't."

"But I haven't got a vehicle, how am I supposed to get rid of it?"

"Not my problem, mate. I don't want to get involved with this shit."

Dick tried to leave the cellar, but Elijah pounced on him, slipped down to his knees and pleaded with him.

"Please, I wouldn't ask you to do this if I wasn't desperate. Please, Dick, help me out."

"It's more than I dare do, Elijah. You're going to have to do this alone."

Elijah buried his head in his hands, mortified by his friend's reluctance to assist him. "They'll deport me. I can't go back. People who return to their native country are treated terribly by the authorities. I'm in a no-win situation here, and none of it is my fault. Please, please won't you reconsider?"

Dick covered his eyes and shook his head. "I understand your dilemma, I truly do... I've got a reputation to uphold, a family to support..."

"I get that and I'm sorry to have to put you in this position, what else can I do? How do you propose I get rid of the body on my own?"

Dick sighed several times and stared at him. "Shit, I'm going to live to regret this, I just know I am."

Elijah got up and ran forward to hug his friend. "I can't thank you enough, your friendship knows no bounds."

"You ever drop me in it, and I'll have no hesitation in blaming you, you hear me?"

"I would never do that. I value our friendship too much. What should we do?"

It was Dick's turn to start pacing. "I need to get out of here for a start, this stench is making me retch. We'll discuss it over a cuppa."

"Yes, that's a great idea."

They ran up the stairs, and Dick closed the door behind him. The smell was better upstairs, only slightly, though. They removed their masks, and both washed their faces at the kitchen sink, doing their best to rid themselves of the excessive odours.

"I can't believe this, I really can't," Dick mumbled over and over as Elijah prepared the mugs of tea. "I think we'd better have our drinks outside." He opened the back door, and the fresh air wafted into the room.

"I should have thought about doing that when I got home. Not sure where my brain is today. It's been a hectic week, and now we have this burning issue to deal with. What are we going to do with the body?"

"We have one thing in our favour, it's dark out there now."

"That's a relief. Where do you think we should put it?"

"We could either dump it in the river or put it in the woods, that's all I can think of right now."

"Yes, yes, that's a good idea, where do you have in mind?" The kettle switched off, and Elijah finished making the drinks and handed a mug to Dick.

Dick led the way into the backyard and lowered his voice in case any of the neighbours overheard him. He clicked his finger and thumb together. "Wayland Wood, it's not too far from here. We can be there and back within forty minutes."

"Should we take spades with us? To bury it?"

Dick waved his hand and shook his head. "Nope, I ain't getting involved in shit like that. It's going to be a matter of driving there, dumping the body, then getting our arses out of there quickly."

"Oh, that's a shame, I think I'll feel bad about not giving the person a proper burial."

"Tough shit, mate. It's either that or I leave now and let you get rid of it by yourself."

"Oh, no! In that case, yes, I think we should do that. I'm so grateful to you, Dick."

"I should think so. Let's hope we don't get caught putting the corpse in the back of the van or at the other end when we dump it."

They both held up their crossed fingers and supped their drinks.

FIFTEEN MINUTES LATER, with the body wrapped in a blanket, they donned a new mask each and ferried the corpse through the house and out to the van. Dick had left the back doors open in readiness. They bundled it in and quietly clicked the doors shut, warily casting a glance around them. Thankfully, the street was quiet and, as far as they knew, they hadn't been seen. They hopped into their seats up front, and Dick drove off.

"Jesus, the stench is filling the van, I'm never going to get rid of it," Dick complained.

"I'm sorry. I'll valet it for you over the weekend, it's the least I can do."

"I'm going to take you up on that offer."

Dick took the next right at the end of the road, out to Watton.

"I've never been out here, it's lovely. Ouch, what am I saying? And we're about to dump a body here; will the locals ever forgive us?"

Dick laughed. "I think that's the least of our worries. Let's just hope no one spots us unloading the van, otherwise… nope, I'm not going there."

"Yes, I agree, let's not worry about what might happen if we get caught. Have I told you how grateful I am, Dick?"

"Once or twice. Hey, you're going to owe me big time for this one, pal."

"Of course, name it and I'll do anything for you in the future, as well as clean your van at the weekend."

"I'll hold you to that."

Dick entered the car park, and they both glanced around them.

"All clear this way. What about you?"

Elijah swiftly nodded and said, "Everything is okay this way."

"Let's get this over and done with then."

They jumped out of the van and ran to the rear of the vehicle.

Dick tore the doors open and reached for one end of the large package, which happened to be the corpse's legs. "Grab the other end, come on, I don't want to draw this out any longer than necessary."

"Give me a chance, it's a bit slippery. I need to get a firm foothold."

Dick rolled his eyes. "You're holding us up. I warned you, this is going to be a quick in-and-out job. Are you ready?"

Elijah held the body by what he assumed were the shoulders, and together, they moved the heavy lump from the back of the van and carried it through the bushes into the woods. Dick held his torch in his mouth, guiding their way, so neither of them spoke until Dick came to a standstill. He lowered his end to the ground and removed the torch.

"This is going to have to do. I can't be bothered to carry it any further."

"What? That's not far at all. We should... Please, Dick, at least another ten feet."

Dick shrugged. "What difference does it make? People are going to smell him before they trip over his body."

"That's true. Okay, maybe you're right. I hate the thought of leaving him here like this."

"Why? It's not like you know him, is it? Or are you holding out on me?"

"Of course I'm not. I told you the truth, I don't know him, and I had no idea there was a body being stored in that freezer. Why don't you believe me?"

"I do. I'm pulling your leg. Where's that naïve sense of humour of yours gone?"

"It's hiding. I no longer feel like smiling. I doubt if I'm ever going to smile again."

Dick flicked his upper arm. "You will. Come on, let's get a wriggle on and get you back home."

They dashed back to the van. Elijah tripped over a large branch and ended up face-first in a muddy patch they had successfully avoided on the way in. Dick placed his hands on his knees and laughed.

"What the… look at me, I'm covered from head to foot now," Elijah complained.

"Forget about it. Get in the van. Don't worry about the mess, you'll be cleaning it up at the weekend anyway." He offered his hand and pulled Elijah to his feet.

They continued their walk back to the van just as a cyclist entered the woods to the right of them.

"Shit, shit, shit. What are we going to do now?" Elijah fretted.

"Get in. We can't worry about him."

Elijah jumped into the passenger seat and stared at Dick during the drive. He looked a very worried man—they both were.

CHAPTER 1

Detective Inspector Sally Parker beeped her horn and drummed her fingers on the steering wheel. Her partner, Lorne Warner, was running late for some reason today, which was totally unlike her. Just as Sally was about to get out of the car to see if everything was all right, Lorne came tearing out of the house. She hitched on her jacket and slipped into the passenger seat.

"I'm soooo sorry. I thought I was going to be on time, but then Tony had a problem with his leg and…"

"I knew there had to be something wrong. Is he all right?"

"I think it's a little infected. Of course, he's telling me otherwise. He's been a touch niggly for the past few days which is always an indication that he's not feeling a hundred percent."

"Funny you should say that because Simon told me last night, over dinner, that Tony hadn't seemed himself for a few days. Why don't you take the day off, and make sure he gets to the doctor's today? His leg won't heal on its own, will it?"

"It's fine. I rang the surgery at eight. I was number ten in the queue. In the time it took for the receptionist to answer my call, I had showered, dried my hair and got dressed. The NHS is really going to pot these days."

"That's disgusting. Did you manage to get an appointment?"

"Yes, at four-thirty this afternoon."

"Good, and you're going to take him. No arguments, you hear me?"

Lorne rolled her eyes. "You're the boss."

"That's right, I am. I know you're worried about him; I'm sure he'll be fine. After all, it's not the first time he's had a flare-up like this, is it?"

"No, but to me, it's happening more frequently these days. That can't be right, which is why I'm having sleepless nights over it, not that I would admit it to him."

Sally started the engine and placed her hand over Lorne's. "I know this is easier said than done but try not to worry too much about him. Hey, at least you've booked an appointment for this afternoon. I caught a report on the news last week that there are people out there who haven't seen their GP in years."

"Disgusting. Hard to believe the NHS has got so bad over the last decade. Okay, this is me pushing it to the back of my mind. What's on the agenda for today?"

"Not a lot at the moment, just completing the paperwork for the last case we solved. The chief wants to see me first thing. I'm hoping it'll be a general chitchat but, in this climate, it could be someone's head he's after."

"Heck, are things that bad?"

"I didn't think so… oh, I don't know. I've been known to talk out of my arse, as you're well aware."

They both laughed. It felt good to ease the tension that had accompanied Lorne when she'd got in the car.

Sally drove to the station. She was a few streets away

when her mobile rang. She answered it using the speaker. "DI Sally Parker."

"Hi, it's Pauline. Any chance you can join me?"

Sally glanced at Lorne, her eyebrows raised. "Of course. Where are you?"

"It's a place called Wayland Wood. Do you know it?"

"I do. We'll be there in around twenty minutes, will that be okay?"

"Let's just say the victim isn't going anywhere anytime soon."

The pathologist ended the call.

"Well, if nothing else, we can call it great timing." Sally smiled and did a U-turn on the quiet road.

"There's always something that comes along to spoil our day. At least it should keep the chief happy."

THEY ARRIVED at the edge of the woods which had been cordoned off, and the only vehicles in the area were two patrol cars and three SOCO vans.

Sally drew up, and the officer on duty at the cordon recognised her. He loosened the tape at one end and gestured for her to enter the car park. She gave him a thumbs-up and, after she passed him, he reattached the tape to the nearby tree.

"We'd better get suited up. Luckily, I stocked the car up the other day as supplies were getting low."

After they'd slipped on their protective clothing, Sally shouted over to the officer who had let them through, "How far is the crime scene?"

"Not too far, ma'am. Take the path straight ahead of you for two to three minutes."

"Thanks."

They carried their protective shoe covers with them, ready to slip them on once they got closer.

"Ah, there you are." Pauline glanced up and acknowledged them. "Come closer, don't be shy."

Taking it in turns to support each other, Sally and Lorne covered their shoes and then made their way towards Pauline. A tech was taking photos of the surrounding area.

"What have we got?" Sally asked.

"A man in his late twenties, possibly early thirties."

Sally crouched beside Pauline, her Tyvek suit rustling as she moved. "What's the cause of death?"

"To be honest with you, I'm not sure yet. I can't find any traces of blood."

Sally frowned and stared at the corpse's face. "Possible strangulation?"

"Maybe, although there doesn't appear to be any marks around his neck."

"What about time of death? Any idea about that?"

"I know this isn't what you want to hear, but I'm unsure. There is no lividity present in the body."

Sally inclined her head. "Meaning?"

"I'd rather not commit right now."

"Come on, Pauline, you've got to give us more than that. What the hell is going on?"

"I took his temperature, and it's only ever happened to me once before."

Sally frowned. "You're confusing me. What are you saying?"

"That I believe the body was most likely to have been frozen before being dumped at this location."

Sally turned to face Lorne who seemed as shocked to hear the news as she was. "I don't think I've ever come across something like this before."

"His core temperature was below average. As the weather

was quite mild last night, there is no reason for his temperature to be that low. I'll know more during the PM; there are certain tests we can carry out."

"Sounds intriguing. So, he was frozen and then dumped at this location. I wonder why. More to the point, is it possible he's been dead for some time?"

"I believe this is going to be a difficult crime to solve. I really can't give you more than that, not until I've got him in theatre."

Sally sighed and nodded. "Okay, in other words, don't push you?"

"Exactly."

They both stood, and a young woman with red hair approached them.

"Ah, Liz, this is DI Sally Parker and her partner, DS Lorne Warner. You'll be seeing a lot of them. This is Liz Owen, she started as my assistant last week. She's still finding her feet, so be gentle with her."

"Don't listen to her, Liz, we always treat the pathology team with respect."

"Occasionally," Pauline muttered behind the clenched fist covering her mouth.

"Uncalled for," Sally replied. "Going back to the victim, have you found any evidence lying around?" She spotted several markers close to the victim's legs.

"A couple of footprints. We'll do the necessary with them, just in case. There's no telling if they're to do with the vic or not. Do you want to be involved in the PM when I finally get him back to the mortuary?"

Sally hitched up a shoulder. "Why not? It's not like we have anything else on at the moment."

"Good. Right, we're almost finished here. Are you going to follow us back or join us later?"

"Depends on what time you're going to conduct the PM."

"I'm clear at the moment, so I'll get cracking on it as soon as we get back, unless something else crops up between now and then, which I doubt."

"I can't believe you said that out loud. I hope you haven't tempted fate."

"Oops, me too."

Sally scanned the area. "Who found the body?"

"The man over to our right, talking to one of your guys. He was on his morning run before work and literally stumbled across the corpse."

"We'll have a word with him. Was the body disguised at all?"

"The body was wrapped in black sacks, which have since been removed."

"I know I'm probably stating the obvious, but there's a foul smell with this one. I take it that's another indication that the body has been frozen, right?"

Pauline applauded her. "Bravo. The lady knows her stuff," she replied.

Sally narrowed her eyes and struggled to work out if Pauline was being condescending or not. She decided not to retaliate and said, "Lorne and I will have a chat with the bloke and then make our way over to the mortuary, if that's all right with you?"

"Sounds like a plan."

Sally and Lorne took a few steps to their right and removed their shoe covers.

"She seemed a bit better towards you today, must be because the pressure is off her shoulders, now she has an assistant working with her," Lorne suggested.

Pauline had been more than a tad tetchy with them both lately, due to the added stress she was under with the department being understaffed.

"We'll see how long that lasts. It might even add to her

stress, depending on how much experience Liz has under her belt."

"True enough. What are you thinking about the crime scene?"

"I'm not, not really. I suppose we need to see what comes up during the PM, first. Strange that Pauline can't give us any indication of what the cause of death is yet," Sally said.

"I haven't come across a corpse being frozen before, so I haven't got a clue what difference it can make to the body."

"I'm sure we'll find out soon enough. Let's see what the witness has to say. He seems somewhat irate, so expect a backlash."

"Maybe we shouldn't hold him up for long if he was running before work."

"I agree. If he's already given his statement, we'll introduce ourselves and let him get on his way."

The man was in his late forties with thinning hair and bright blue eyes.

"Hi, I'm DI Sally Parker, and this is DS Lorne Warner. Are you up to answering a few questions for us… Mr?"

"Bartlett. Not again. I've gone over this three times already. I've just given my statement, isn't that good enough these days? I'm late for work as it is."

"I'm sorry, Mr Bartlett, I'll make this as brief as possible."

He huffed out a breath and folded his arms. After a few moments, he began tapping his foot as if emphasising his point. "Get on with it then."

Sally held out her hand for the statement, and the attending officer passed her his clipboard. She briefly scanned through it and then asked, "Were you alone when you found the body?"

"Yes. What type of question is that? I always run alone."

"And do you run here every morning, sir?" Sally asked.

"Every other day. I prefer to vary the routes I take to

prevent the boredom from setting in. All the details are there, in my statement."

"I'm sorry, I won't hold you up much longer. As you can imagine, the need to question witnesses at the scene can be crucial to solving the crime."

"I understand that, but as I told your colleague, I saw nothing. I stumbled across the body and reported it as soon as I got my breath back, and then I waited for the patrol car to arrive. That was nearly an hour ago now and, as I've already stated, I'm late for work."

"I appreciate that, Mr Bartlett. One last question and then you're free to go."

"Make it quick, Inspector."

"Did you see anyone else hanging around? Or were there any vehicles parked close by when you arrived?"

"No, and no. I was alone in the woods, just like I am on other mornings, which is why I prefer to come here first thing. I've tried running in the evening, and this place can be quite busy, the lack of spaces in the car park doesn't help, either. I don't suppose you can do anything about that for the regulars, can you?"

Sally smiled. "I can see what I can do. It is a beautiful area for you to choose for your run."

"It is. Is that it?"

Sally nodded. "You're free to go. Thank you for sparing the time to go over your statement with us. I'll give you one of my cards. Should you think of anything else you've forgotten to put in your statement, don't hesitate to get in touch with me."

She handed him a card. He took it and popped it into his bum bag.

"I won't be adding anything because there is nothing else to add, Inspector. Now, if you'll excuse me, I must jog on, and yes, the pun was intended."

"Thanks for your help," she called after him. "Leave the statement with the desk sergeant if you would, I'll collect it when we get back to the station," she told the officer.

They strolled back to the corpse but kept their distance.

"Hmm... okay, that's something I didn't notice before." Lorne pointed at the man's shoes. "Aren't they similar to the ones Simon wears?"

Sally nodded. "Good spot. They're really expensive. I think the last pair he bought cost him nearly two thousand quid."

"Ouch, fifty quid is our limit for shoes."

"You're not alone there." Lorne's observation made Sally give the body the once-over again, if only from a distance. "Is that a watch he's wearing, Pauline?"

"It is. I wasn't going to remove it until I got back to base."

"Would you mind?" Sally grinned, warding off any feistiness she expected to come her way.

"If you insist." Pauline removed the watch from the victim's wrist and read the back. "There's an inscription. 'To our darling son, love Mum and Dad.'"

"Helpful... not. I was at least hoping for a name to be engraved on there."

"Looks like we're going to have to solve this case the hard way." Lorne groaned.

"As per usual. Are you going to be long?" Sally asked Pauline and then glanced at her watch. It was already nine-thirty.

"Another ten minutes or so. Am I holding you up?"

"Not at all. I need to make a call to the station. We'll be waiting in the car and will follow you when you set off."

"Suits me."

Liz appeared with an evidence bag, and Pauline dropped the watch into it.

Back at the cordon, Sally and Lorne stripped off their

suits and deposited them in the black sack. In the car, Sally rang the station. Joanna answered the phone.

"Hi, boss. We were wondering where you'd got to. Everything all right?"

"Yes, we received a call on our way in and changed direction to attend a crime scene. We're following the pathologist back to the mortuary to attend the PM."

"Really? That's unusual. May I ask why?"

Sally chuckled. "I'd think something was up if you didn't. The pathologist believes the victim might have been frozen before being dumped in the woods."

"Oh shit. Sorry, ugh, that doesn't sound good. Is there anything we can be doing at this end, or is it too early to ask that?"

"What we have so far is this: the victim was wearing Louis Vuitton loafers and had a watch with an inscription on it. No names mentioned, obviously a present from his mother and father."

"Where do we begin with this one?" Joanna asked.

"Right now, I'm not really sure trawling through the MisPers list is going to help us."

"It's a tough one, especially if you don't have a clue of how long he was missing, or if he was ever reported missing. The gift from his parents could have been made years ago and they might have died since."

"Yep, that's a distinct possibility. Anyway, I just wanted to touch base with you, and let you know what was going on and that we weren't skiving today."

"As if. Umm... where was the body found?" Joanna asked.

"Wayland Wood, do you know it?"

"I do. Rumour has it that's where the *Babes in the Wood* story originated from."

"Wow, they say you learn something new every day. I wasn't aware of that fact, thanks, Joanna."

"You're welcome. I'm full of useless information like that. We'll see you when we see you, then."

"You will."

The SOCO and pathologist team ferried their equipment back to the vans and then returned with a stretcher for the corpse. The corpse was zipped up in a full-length body bag and placed in the back of one of the vans. The convoy left the parking lot. Sally joined them to bring up the rear. The mortuary was around thirty minutes away.

After pulling on another protective suit and slipping on their calf-length wellies, Sally and Lorne joined Pauline, Liz and another tech in the theatre. The stench from the body was now unbearable.

"Any chance we can wear a mask with a filter, to prevent us from wanting to vomit every five minutes?"

Pauline nodded at Liz who then wandered off to collect two masks sitting on a nearby trolley.

"Thanks, these should do the trick." Sally smiled at Liz.

"Let's hope so. Granted, the smell is awful, far worse than normal." Liz returned to her position, standing off to the side of Pauline, ready to jump in and lend a hand if needed.

"Right, why don't we make a start? I'm going to open him up and get the relevant samples from his liver; that's going to confirm if he's been frozen or not."

"Can I ask how? Only because neither Lorne nor I have come across this type of thing before."

"We need to measure the activity of short-chain 3-hydroxyacyl-CoA dehydrogenase."

"Crap, I wish I hadn't asked now."

Pauline grinned.

"As a matter of interest, how long does a cadaver take to thaw?" Sally asked.

"Approximately twenty-four hours," Pauline replied. She continued to insert the scalpel to make the Y-shaped incision. "While you were getting changed, I took a sample of skin which I then studied under the microscope, and can indeed confirm that the body has been frozen and thawed. You're going to ask me how I know that, aren't you?"

Sally and Lorne both nodded.

"Frozen tissue has distinct damage when viewed under the microscope—ice crystals form within the cells and rupture the cell membranes, causing catastrophic structural failure. Lysosomes are also ruptured in the process, denaturing many proteins and turning tissues to 'mush'. When you compare tissues that were frozen to non-frozen, the visual appearance is unmistakable."

"It isn't the first time I've said this today, you learn something new every day."

Pauline's brow furrowed. "What am I missing?"

"Nothing, it's just something a member of my team revealed when I told her the location of the crime scene."

"Are you going to keep me in the dark?"

"Wayland Wood is where the *Babes in the Wood* story originated."

Pauline raised a finger. "That's correct, I learnt that myself about five years ago. A fascinating fact."

"Maybe leaving the body there was intentional," Sally suggested.

Pauline pulled a face. "You reckon? Are you aware of the facts regarding the *Babes in the Wood* story?"

Sally grimaced. "I'll keep quiet until I do my research and get back to you."

Pauline chuckled. "You do that."

"As this is all new to us, can you explain things further? By that I mean, are there any other ways of knowing if a body has been frozen then thawed?"

"Let's see, ah yes, one of the most common methods is to examine the blood for the presence of ice crystals. When a body is frozen, ice crystals can form in the blood, which can be seen under a microscope. Additionally, we'll also carry out tests for changes in the red blood cells, such as an increase in the number of cells or a decrease in their size."

"Interesting. Maybe we should attend PMs more often," Sally responded. "What do you reckon, Lorne?"

"When I was in London, I enjoyed—maybe that's the wrong word to use—but I often attended PMs and was eager to do so. It's surprising what facts you pick up along the way," Lorne said.

Sally held a hand to her mouth and whispered, "That wouldn't have anything to do with a certain Jacques Arnaud, would it?"

Lorne's cheeks coloured up, and she tutted. "I should have known you'd throw that one at me."

"Sorry, I couldn't resist."

"If you're quite finished, ladies," Pauline chastised them.

Sally cringed. "Sorry, as you were."

Pauline kept them informed with how the process was faring during the rest of the examination and, at the end of the lengthy post-mortem, she confirmed that her initial diagnosis was right.

"Can you tell how he was killed?" Sally stared at the inner workings of the corpse.

"Hard to say. I found no evidence of any wounds on the body. Again, if you pushed me for an answer, I would say the victim was probably rendered unconscious and then shoved in the freezer to allow hypothermia to take hold. There are no signs of excessive force across his mouth, so I don't believe he was gagged."

"Any wounds to the back of the head? Giving us a clue as to whether he was attacked from behind or not?"

"None, from what I could tell. We'll take samples of his

organs and carry out the usual tests, that should tell us if he was poisoned. It's all rather mysterious, isn't it?"

"You're not wrong. Can you give us his height and approximate weight? We're going to need something concrete to help us wade through the missing person files," Sally asked.

Pauline nodded and reached for the tape sitting on the trolley beside her. "I can give you his height and a guesstimate of his weight. Liz, can you grab the other end for me?"

Liz rushed to assist Pauline. She held the metal end and walked the length of the table to the corpse's feet.

"In old money, he's six feet two inches," Pauline glanced up and said, "and I'd say he was around twelve stone."

"That's brilliant, hopefully, something will come to light when we search the files. Anything else we should be aware of? Any birthmarks or distinctive tattoos?"

"Nothing that I could see."

"Can I check his clothes?" Lorne asked.

"Fill your boots," Pauline replied.

Lorne crossed the room and snapped on a pair of latex gloves. She held up the man's jeans and shirt which had both been cut from his body.

"What are you thinking?" Sally approached her and asked.

"Well, judging by the shoes he was wearing, I thought it would be an idea to see if his clothes had designer labels as well."

"Ah, yes, and do they?"

Lorne held up the garments, so the labels were showing. "Gucci jeans and the shirt is by Ralph Lauren. So yes, I'd say he had expensive tastes."

Sally fished her phone out of her pocket and took a couple of photos of the clothing. "What about the watch?"

"I've given that to the tech boys. Maybe catch them on

your way out?" Pauline said. "Can I get on with the pressing matter of completing the PM now?"

Lorne and Sally returned to their positions on the other side of the table, and Lorne mumbled an apology.

Pauline concluded the PM without further interruption from either Sally or Lorne.

"Will you let me know ASAP what the results are from the samples you've taken today?"

"What, you mean like I always do?" Pauline smirked.

"Sorry. I want to take a photo of the watch, just in case we have to go down the press conference route."

"Feel free. I'll be in touch soon."

Sally and Lorne headed back to the changing rooms, removed their protective clothing and slipped on their boots. They left the changing room and walked back up the hallway, stopping at the last door near the exit.

"Hi, Pauline left a watch with you guys from this morning's crime scene."

The tech left his workbench and exited the room only to return a few seconds later carrying the watch in an evidence bag. He pointed at the box of latex gloves on his workbench. "You'd better glove up before you touch it."

"Of course. I won't keep you too long. I need to take some photos for a press conference I'll probably need to call in order for us to identify the body."

"In that case, allow me." He removed the watch from the bag and angled it in different positions while Sally took her photos. "Have you got enough now?" he asked.

Sally checked the images she'd captured and smiled. "That's perfect. Thanks for your help."

The tech put the watch back in the bag and fastened it. "It's all part of the service."

. . .

BACK AT THE STATION, they found the rest of the team hard at work.

"I'll get the coffees," Lorne said. "Does anyone else want one while I'm at it?"

Their colleagues shook their heads.

"We've not long had one," Joanna replied. "How did the PM go?"

Sally shrugged and collapsed into the chair next to Joanna. "It went. It's a waiting game now. The pathologist couldn't tell us what the cause of death was. Her main suspicion is that the victim was poisoned, possibly."

"That's unusual," Joanna replied. "We've been going through the Missing Person files, although I didn't know how far to go back."

Sally sighed. "Regrettably, we still don't know. All we've got to go on is that the victim was dressed from head to foot in designer clothes."

Lorne handed Sally her drink. "We have no idea if this man was local or not. For all we know, he might have been attending a meeting or some kind of conference in the area. So, it would be remiss of us not to broaden the search."

"I can get on with that right away," Joanna said.

"Before you do, the pathologist confirmed his height as being six-two and his weight around twelve stone," Lorne said.

"Excellent, that should whittle the list down significantly."

Sally rose from her seat and walked towards her office. "I'll get on with my chores but first I'll give Georgia a call. Ask her if there's any chance of holding a conference today before the press find out about the discovery and run with the story."

"Makes sense," Lorne said. "Is there anything specific you want me to do?"

"Nothing, except help with the search."

"I'll do that."

Sally opened the door to her office and groaned at the number of envelopes sitting in her in-tray, and that was without starting up her computer to check how many emails she had received overnight. She set the chore to one side to make her urgent call. "Hi, Georgia, long time no hear, it's Sally Parker."

"Hello, Inspector. I was only thinking about you the other day… oops, I hope that didn't come across as me being stalkerish."

Sally laughed. "It didn't. How are you fixed today?"

"Me personally? Or did you mean conference-wise?"

"The latter, although I suspect you're going to tell me the two things go hand in hand."

"They do. Thus far, I'm all clear for the day. May I ask why?"

"We were called out to a crime scene first thing. We've subsequently attended the PM of the victim and we're none the wiser about his identity. I don't want this information to get out yet, but the pathologist believes that he was frozen after his death."

"Oh shit. Wow, I can't recall having to deal with a case like that before. Yes, of course, I can summon the press to attend. What time were you thinking?"

"The earlier the better. My team are trawling through the missing persons database but, as yet, nothing has come to light. You know how many times they've had to do that over the last couple of years, I'm assuming something would have stood out by now."

"I agree. Maybe he was from out of the area."

"That's the conclusion we've recently come to, so my team are widening the search. The thing is, the victim was wearing a Rolex watch; the inscription on the back doesn't mention a name, but it was from his parents."

"Well, that's a start. Okay, let me see what I can arrange and get back to you. It shouldn't take too long."

"You're amazing. Thanks, Georgia."

Sally ended the call and knuckled down to tackle the envelopes, but not before she'd finished the rest of her coffee. Georgia called back thirty minutes later to confirm she'd arranged a conference for two that afternoon. Sally thanked her and confirmed the arrangements with the team.

"That doesn't give us much time," Lorne said.

"I understand, but we need to get the details out there about the watch. Have you found anything yet?"

"Nothing at all."

Sally groaned and returned to her chores, unable to get the victim's face out of her mind. She already felt she was failing him. It was a silly idea, given how long they'd been on the case, but she had a niggling doubt running through her that there was more to his death and that they were about to uncover yet another investigation that was built on a web of lies.

Sally met up with Georgia at ten minutes to two in the anteroom. "I've been considering your case since you got in touch with me, and I have to tell you, it's made me shudder a few times."

"Thought it might. You wouldn't want to have witnessed the body first hand, the stench was appalling; no disrespect to the victim, it was hardly his fault."

"Do you know how long he's been dead?"

"No, that's a mystery in itself. We've got very little to go on so far, that's why I thought it would be best to get the conference out of the way early. My team are doing their very best up there, but even they have their limits. There were a few footprints but no other evidence was found at the scene. We're aware the victim had money, judging by the clothes and shoes he was wearing. Of course, that's not always the case, and I've known some people that live beyond their means just to impress their friends and family."

"Interesting. Okay, let's see what the journalists think of it all."

"Do we have to?" Sally laughed, a sudden wave of reluctance overwhelming her.

"Come on, you'll be fine. I'll be right there beside you."

"I feel better already."

Georgia led the way through to the conference room, and they took up their seats behind the long table. Sally, feeling embarrassed under the spotlight, poured them both a glass of water as the murmuring died down in the room.

"First of all, I'd like to thank you all for attending this conference today at such short notice. In a moment it will become apparent why one has been called in at short notice. Without further ado, I'll hand the reins over to Detective Inspector Sally Parker."

Lights flashed, and Sally gulped down another sip of water before she spoke. "I echo what Ms Neves said, thank you all for attending at short notice. My partner and I were called out to a crime scene by the local pathologist this morning. The victim was a man in his early thirties, height six-two and weight around twelve stone."

"Do you have a photo of the victim?" a young male journalist asked from the middle of the pack.

"I do, but there are reasons why I can't share that with you right now. We do, however, have the victim's watch in our possession. It's pretty distinctive, a Rolex with an inscription on the back that says, 'To our darling son, love Mum and Dad'. Unfortunately, the victim's name wasn't used, which would have given us a significant lead to go on."

"What else can you tell us, Inspector?" the same journalist asked.

"Can you refrain from asking questions until the end? Let the inspector finish what she has to share with you first. Thank you," Georgia said, jumping in before Sally could answer.

The journalist held his head in shame, and Sally nudged Georgia's knee under the table to thank her. She wasn't at her best once her momentum went awry, and Georgia was aware of that fact.

"At this stage, because of an important piece of evidence, we discovered about the man's death, which I must apologise for in advance, I can't reveal yet, we have no knowledge as to how long the man has been dead or when he actually went missing. We're trawling through our missing persons database at present, but that's proving difficult. So, the reason I decided to call a conference this early into the investigation, was to plead for the public's help to identify the victim."

Sally had already given Georgia a copy of the photos she'd taken of the watch and the man's shoes, and Georgia hit a button on the desk to begin the slide show.

"This is the watch we found on the victim. Does anyone recognise it? If you do, can you call the number at the bottom of your screen? Sadly, that's all I can give you for now. Please, if you recognise this watch or these shoes, get in touch with us as soon as possible. Thank you for your time."

"The inspector is now open to answering your questions," Georgia said.

The same journalist raised his hand.

Georgia pointed to him. "Yes, go ahead, Vince."

"His shoes are an expensive make, even I can recognise them as Louis Vuitton's. What about the rest of his clothes, or was the victim found naked?"

"Good question, he was found wearing a Ralph Lauren shirt and Gucci trousers."

"Great, and are you prepared to tell us where the body was discovered?"

"Around seven this morning, by a runner out at Wayland Wood."

"Ah, the infamous woodland, and you say there was no further evidence found at the scene? Any vehicles seen leaving the area by the witness?"

"Sadly not. That's all we have at this time."

"Do you think the victim was killed on site or possibly transported to the location after his death?"

"We're unsure. I'm inclined to believe the latter but I'm not going to commit one hundred percent to that."

"And what happens if a member of the public doesn't come forward? How are you going to solve the case then, Inspector?"

Sally smiled at the journalist who was intent on unnerving her. "Hopefully it won't come to that. As I've already stated, the victim was only discovered this morning, meaning that the investigation is still in its infancy. We're aware of how these types of cases progress. My team are the best at sourcing clues that other teams in the Force often dismiss or totally miss altogether."

"I've heard your reputation is second to none and that the Cold Case Team leaves no stone unturned during an investigation, Inspector, is that right?"

"That's correct. Are there any further questions?"

"Just one." The same journalist raised his hand again.

Sally nodded for him to continue.

"How is your husband doing now?"

Sally grimaced and inclined her head. "I prefer to keep my personal life private. Anything else?" she asked, her gaze flitting around the room.

"I only ask because I know he had a few problems with his property development business not long ago. Didn't you and your team have to come to his rescue?"

"I meant any other questions relating to this investigation."

"Aren't you going to answer me?" the journalist probed.

Georgia stepped in and ended the conference, using her usual spiel to thank them for their time, and then she and Sally left the room.

"What an utter tosser. How the hell did he find out about that? If my senior officers hear about this…"

Georgia rubbed Sally's upper arm. "I doubt if they will. What happened?"

Sally closed her eyes and shook her head. "Simon and Tony had a run-in with another property developer. Things turned nasty; he damaged Simon's car before turning his attention to some of the properties that had been renovated and were due to be put on the market. It was all rather messy at the end. My ex-partner, Jack, who is now a PI, called for backup at one of the properties. We showed up in force and took this bloke down; he's currently serving time."

"Ouch, I had no idea about this, Sally. Was anyone hurt?"

"Not really. A few bruises here and there, but if Jack hadn't made the call, I dread to think what might have happened if we hadn't shown up. The guy, for want of a better word, was a thug."

"That's not good. Glad you were able to jump in and rescue hubby before any real damage was done."

"Me, too. We're over it now, and the guy is sitting in prison; justice prevailed in the end. How do you think the conference went?"

"Fine, considering you couldn't tell them much. Let's hope it reaches the victim's family and they get in touch with you soon."

Sally held up her crossed fingers. "I hope that's the case, too. Right, I'd better get back to it. Thanks for going above and beyond, as usual, Georgia."

"It's always a pleasure. Let me know if anything comes from the conference, won't you? I can add it to my résumé."

Sally frowned. "What? You're not thinking of leaving, are you?"

"Oh no, it's just something I've always done. It doesn't do any harm to keep a record of your successes, does it?"

Sally exhaled a breath. "Blimey, you had me worried then. I suppose you're right. Anyway, I'd better get back to it. Speak soon."

CHAPTER 2

As it was, the conference aired that night, but the response was lacklustre to say the least. It wasn't until a couple of days later that Sally received a call from a distraught woman.

"Hello, DI Sally Parker, how may I help you?"

"I don't know if you're the person I should be speaking to or not."

"Why don't you tell me what's on your mind, Mrs...?"

"Sorry, yes. I'm Alice Jessop. I've been away for the week on a short break with my husband to celebrate our fortieth anniversary and when I got back my neighbour asked me if I had seen the news regarding a watch that had been found."

Sally sat upright and plucked a piece of paper from her tray and picked up her pen. "I see. Did you manage to see the news bulletin yourself on catch-up?"

"Oh no, that's foolish of me, I never thought to do that. Do you want me to do that first and call you back?"

"No, no, it's fine. I can come out and visit you, if that's all right?"

"Yes, that would be perfect. You'll be wanting my address then."

"Please."

"It's forty-five Windy Lane in Acle. Do you know the area at all?"

"Yes, I'm local, I've lived here all my life. I'll head off now, I should be with you in say half an hour."

"Oh my, I'd better give this place the once-over before you arrive then. I had lots of washing to do when I came back, and the weather hasn't been very good, so I couldn't hang it out."

Sally sniggered. "Sounds like my house. Please don't worry on my account."

"Awful, isn't it? And I hate using those damn tumble driers."

"Me, too. I often receive electric shocks every time I use mine, so I've given up. I'll see you soon."

"Thank you."

Sally left her office and informed the rest of the team. "Are you ready to head over there, Lorne?"

Her partner nodded and removed her jacket from the back of the chair.

"I'll get my things together and we'll shoot off."

THE HOUSE WAS A THATCHED COTTAGE, situated halfway up Windy Lane. "Stunning. I've always loved cottages, especially in this area," Sally said.

"I agree picture-postcard perfect and look at that garden. Someone spends a considerable amount of time tending to that every day."

"It's amazing. Roll on retirement, eh?"

Lorne chuckled. "For you maybe, I'll still have the dogs to see to. I don't think I'll ever stop rescuing dogs in need, and let's face it, times are tougher than ever right now, despite what the government are telling us."

"I concur. Right, let's get in there, and see what Mrs Jessop can tell us about the victim, if anything."

They left the car and walked up the herringbone-tiled path. The door opened before Sally got the chance to ring the bell.

"Hello, I saw you get out of your car. I'm Alice Jessop."

Sally and Lorne flashed their warrant cards, and Sally made the introductions.

"Do come in, ladies. Can I get you a cup of tea or coffee?"

"Coffee would be lovely," Sally replied. "Both milk with one sugar, thank you."

"I think we'll be better off in the kitchen; I fear the washing has defeated me and is strewn all over the lounge at present."

Sally smiled. "The kitchen will be fine, Alice."

The room was like something out of *Country Life* magazine. It was obviously an extension to the property. It was subtle but exquisite all the same. Oak beams and posts were dotted around the room. It wasn't just a kitchen, there was a dining table and chairs to the left and a comfy snug area with a TV off to the right. Behind that were bi-fold doors that led out to a colourful garden. The lawn was a lush green, not a dandelion in sight.

"This is beautiful, have you lived here long?" Sally asked.

"Thank you. Around thirty years. This area was added about five years ago. We're delighted with how it turned out and tend to spend most of our time in here during the summer, mainly because we're in and out of the garden all the time."

"Both the house and the garden are a credit to you and your husband. Is he here?"

"Yes, umm… not right now. I asked him to nip to the shop

because I didn't have any cake. I can't welcome strangers into my home and offer you a drink without a slice of cake on the side."

"You're too kind. You shouldn't have bothered."

With that, an elderly man wearing a straw hat and chinos walked through the back door. "Sorry, I thought I'd be home sooner. The shop was a hive of activity. A teenager was caught shoplifting and the police arrived to take him away. Poor Meg was beside herself as the teenager hit her with a can of tomatoes and threatened to rob the till. Luckily, Jed Tinker was in the shop at the time and came to Meg's rescue. He wrestled the youth to the floor and pinned him down until the patrol car arrived."

"Oh my. I'll give her a call later, to see how she is. Never mind that for now, Ian, this is DI Sally Parker and her partner, DS Laura Warner."

Lorne smiled. "It's Lorne, but an easy mistake to make."

"Gosh, I'm not that clever with names at my age. Sorry." She took the cake from her husband. "Would you like some? It's our favourite, cherry."

"Hard to refuse on an empty stomach," Sally said.

"Why don't you show the officers to the snug area, Ian? I won't be long."

"I'll wash my hands first. I didn't get a chance to do it before I was ordered to go to the shop."

"Don't worry about us. Shall we take a seat?" Sally pointed at the comfy chairs on the right.

"Yes, do that. We'll be with you shortly."

Sally and Lorne crossed the room as Mrs Jessop continued to issue her husband with orders while he washed his hands at the sink.

After five minutes of clattering plates, cups and saucers, the Jessops joined them with their coffees and pieces of cherry cake. Alice handed Sally and Lorne a side plate and a cup and saucer each.

Sally smiled. "This looks delicious, it's not every day we get spoilt like this."

"The police deserve to be treated with respect. Where would we be without your hard work in keeping this country safe? A timely reminder after what's just happened to Meg."

"We do our best." Sally paused a moment or two and then said, "You mentioned something about a watch on the phone."

The couple glanced at each other and then back at her.

"That's right," Alice said quietly. "We have a suspicion that it might belong to our son."

"Can I ask what makes you think that?" Sally took a sip from her coffee, surprised by the richness of the blend.

"Dan went missing nearly two years ago."

"And I take it you haven't heard from him since?"

"No. Dan would never have intentionally lost touch with us. He was as devoted to us as we were to him. Do you have the watch?"

Sally withdrew her phone from her jacket pocket, scrolled through her images and stopped at the one she regarded as the best one she'd taken of the watch and showed it to the couple. Alice instantly broke down when she saw it.

"Yes, that's right, isn't it, Ian?"

With tears in his eyes, her husband nodded. "Yes. Do you have a photo of the inscription on the back?"

Sally flipped through to the next photo.

Alice reached for her husband's hand. "Yes, that's definitely his. I can't believe it. Two years we've sat here and wondered every day where he'd gone, and all the time… he was probably dead."

"At the moment, we have no way of knowing how long ago your son died."

"May we ask why?" Ian asked.

"Because, although Dan was found in the woods a few days ago, what I neglected to reveal during the press conference was that his body was in the process of thawing."

Again, the Jessops exchanged puzzled glances before Ian asked, "Thawing? Are you telling us that he'd been frozen?"

"That's what the pathologist believes. We attended the post-mortem hours after the body was discovered, and the pathologist carried out several tests on the corpse's organs which confirmed your son, if it is your son, had been frozen."

Alice sobbed, and Ian comforted her with an arm wrapped around the shoulder, then he gently rocked her. "How? Who would do such a thing? Is that how he died?"

"We're still awaiting the cause of death; the pathologist is still waiting on some results coming back from the lab before she'll commit. Do you have a photo of your son from around the time he went missing?"

Ian rose from his seat and walked out of the room. He returned carrying a large silver-framed photo and showed it to Sally, who angled it so Lorne could see at the same time.

"Yes, I believe we're talking about the same person. I don't suppose you have anything of his here that we can take a DNA sample from?"

"Such as?" Ian asked.

"A toothbrush or a comb perhaps. Failing that, if you can tell us who his dentist was, we can visit them and obtain his records."

"Yes, visiting the dentist would be the best thing to do," Ian agreed. "It's the same one we use, Acle Dental Practice."

"We'll get in touch with them when we leave here. I know this has probably come as a huge shock to you both, but are you up to answering some questions for us?"

"Of course. If you think we can help. We want to do what

we can, for our son's sake," Alice replied, her voice catching in her throat.

"I'm going to ask you to cast your mind back to the week or so before your son went missing. Did he mention if he was in any kind of trouble at all?"

Alice stared at her husband and shook her head. "I can't think of anything, can you?"

"No, not that I can remember, not at this time," Ian confirmed. "How do you think he was killed? If he was frozen, where was he kept? In a commercial freezer or a home freezer?" He closed his eyes and shuddered after asking the question.

"That's what we need to find out. Perhaps you wouldn't mind telling us a little about your son's background?"

Lorne withdrew her notebook.

"What's there to tell? He was quite successful, he used to be an estate agent a few years ago, until he got fed up with sitting on his backside all day. He took out a loan from the bank and bought a second property. It needed slight renovations, so he cracked on with that. Then he put it back on the market and made thirty thousand from the sale, *after* all the necessary fees had been taken out. That gave him an appetite to do more, so he approached the bank for a larger loan, which enabled him to buy a bigger house. Again, he completed the renovations; he already knew the builder from his time as an estate agent. They made a pretty good team. They were able to turn the second house around within a month or so, and he made another huge profit on it."

"So, what you're telling us is that he had an eye for a bargain," Sally said.

"Yes, he carried on buying and flipping the houses for a couple of years, always carefully setting the profit he made from one house to the next until he could afford a decent one of his own to live in. Up until then, he'd always lived with us. That's how we were able to make the renovations to this place because we had his rent coming in."

"So, he bought his own house before he passed. Where was that?"

"Not far from here in Brundall, close enough for him to pop by and see us when he wanted a decent meal. His girlfriend wasn't the best in the kitchen."

"Wait, he had a girlfriend?" Sally asked, her interest nudging up a notch.

"Yes, not that we've seen her since he disappeared. We always found her to be rather strange. Maybe that's the wrong word… What do you think, love?" Ian asked his wife.

"I'd say she was always distant. We tried our utmost to get to know her better, so did Dan, but quite often she point blank refused to visit us. Dan would regularly show up on his own. He always made excuses for her absence, she was either running late at work, she'd just enrolled in a bookkeeping class at college, or she was on a night out with the girls because it was one of her friends' birthdays. You know the type of thing. In the end, we accepted it. As long as she didn't prevent our son from visiting us, it really didn't matter what she got up to."

"And after your son went missing, did you visit her?"

"Yes, actually, if I remember rightly, she was the one who rang us, asking if he was here. When we told her we hadn't seen him for a few days, she hung up. Alice and I decided to go round there to see her, and we found her in tears. Alice made her a drink to calm her down, it appeared to work, too, but then we started questioning her and she got angry. Told us that she and Dan had argued and he'd walked out on her."

"Okay, we're going to need to speak with her. Sorry, I didn't catch her name."

"Vanessa. I can't tell you her surname, sorry," Ian said.

"I can't remember it either," Alice replied.

"Did she live with your son?"

"Yes, she moved in not long after he bought the house."

"Is she still there?"

"No. We went through a rough time emotionally and physically around the time our son went missing. Alice was diagnosed with breast cancer."

"I'm so sorry to hear that. Did you receive chemo?"

"I did. It took a lot out of me, as you can imagine. Kept us very occupied but didn't stop us worrying about our son."

"Do you know where Vanessa is now?"

They both shook their heads and then Alice glanced up and announced, "I think her surname was Kitten, if that helps?"

"It does. Thank you. Do you know what happened to the house?"

"Yes, we sold it, put the money aside for our son in case he ever returned. She wanted to stay there but couldn't afford the bills, not that she told us that at the beginning. We let her live there for six months and went round one day to find bailiffs on the doorstep. She pleaded with us to help her out. We paid the debts she had incurred and then ordered her to pack her bags and get out of our son's house. She went, and we haven't heard a word from her since. The ungrateful madam owes us five thousand two hundred pounds. We had to dip into our life savings, our pension pot, to help her out when her parents refused to step in and help. We shouldn't have done it but that's the way we are, unselfish to the core, apparently."

Sally smiled. "I can tell that you're kind people. What was their relationship like, did Dan ever mention?"

"Not really. We think he was happy enough. Hard to say. We've never been the type to interfere in our son's relationships… Will we get the chance to say goodbye to him?" Alice asked, her question coming after a slight pause.

"Yes, I can give you the pathologist's number. We'll need to make a formal identification, if you're up for that?"

"Oh yes. We appreciate how difficult it is going to be to see him, but at least it will give us a chance to say goodbye properly, something that we haven't been able to do up until now."

"I can understand that. As long as you're up to it, no pressure from either the pathologist or us; we can use the dental records to identify your son if you think it's going to be too much for you."

"No, we'd rather do it ourselves, wouldn't we, Ian?"

"Yes, he deserves that."

"If you give me your phone number, I'll call the pathologist when we leave, tell her to get in touch with you."

Ian nodded and gave his wife's shoulders a squeeze. "Will we be able to see him today?"

"Probably. Do you want me to call her now?"

"If you don't mind," Ian replied.

Sally placed her cup and saucer and her empty plate on the tray in front of her and stood. She crossed the room and dialled Pauline's number. "Hey, I'm glad I've caught you. The good news is that we believe we've identified the victim who was found in the woods the other day."

"That's great news. Who?"

"Dan Jessop. Lorne and I are here with his parents now… umm… they're asking to see him. Is that possible yet?"

"Absolutely, give me a couple of hours to get the latest PM out of the way and I'm all theirs."

"What if I tell them to drop by at about two? Does that suit you?"

"It does. Any background for me?"

"Not really. He was a property developer. As soon as we leave here, we're going to try and track down the girlfriend he was living with, at the time of his disappearance. The parents can't think of why anyone would want to hurt or kill their son."

"I'm sure it will come to light soon enough. Glad you've managed to find the parents. Was that because of the conference?"

"Yes, they've been away for a few days. Their neighbour informed them about the watch, and they rang me this morning."

"I'm pleased they reached out to you, otherwise this case might have lingered on the 'unsolved' pile for a while."

"You're not wrong. Okay, I'm going to crack on now. I'll ask them to visit you at two, as agreed."

"Please do. Well done, Sally."

"Thanks, Pauline. Speak later." Sally ended the call, pleased that she and Pauline had finally appeared to put their differences aside, for now at least. Only time would tell if that was a permanent situation or not. She returned to Lorne and the Jessops to share the news. "All sorted. Can you be at the mortuary for two this afternoon?"

"Without a doubt. Thank you for making the arrangements, Inspector," Alice replied.

"My pleasure. Is there anything else you can add before we leave?"

"I don't think so. What about you, Ian?"

"No, not really. I just want to assure you that our son was a good man, he wasn't the type to get into trouble. He's never caused us any form of concern with his behaviour during his thirty-two years on this earth. He enjoyed living a full life, had a penchant for the good things, like clothes and shoes, but he worked damn hard to achieve that sort of lifestyle, unlike some of the youngsters today."

"Thank you, it's information like that which can be valuable to an investigation. You stay there, we'll show ourselves out. Oh, and I'll leave you one of my cards. Don't hesitate to call me day or night if you have any questions."

She handed the card to Alice.

"Thank you for this, and for being so kind to us. I was dreading having to deal with the police today, but you've both made the process painless."

"It's been a pleasure meeting you both, so sorry it had to be under these circumstances. My team and I will be working hard to get you both the answers and justice you need over the coming weeks."

"Will you keep us informed about how the investigation is proceeding?" Ian asked. He rose to his feet.

"If anything significant comes to light, yes, I'll be in touch with you."

"I'll show you out. I'm not one for sitting on my backside all day. I get cramps in my legs if I sit down for too long, don't I, love?" Ian stated.

"So true, neither of us can sit still for too long."

"I can imagine. Someone has to keep on top of that beautiful garden of yours."

"We're both out there tinkering, long into the evening most days. It's our greatest pleasure in life," Ian said.

He smiled at his wife, and Alice confirmed with a smile and a nod.

"It has stopped us thinking over the years. When Dan first disappeared, we both sat here all day, moping, wondering where he was. We're not very good at detective work so didn't know where to begin, and the copper we reported him missing to gave us the impression that he wasn't going to do much to help us."

"I'm sorry you were treated that way. I want to assure you

that we won't stop until we get all the answers about your son's death."

Ian led the way to the front door. He opened it and stretched out his hand for them to shake. "We have confidence in you both. Thank you for coming to see us today. Please do your best to find the person responsible for robbing us of our son."

"You have my word, we're going to give it our all. Take care of each other."

"We will, we're all we've got now."

Sally smiled. She and Lorne left the house and walked back to the car.

"Nice couple. Shame we had to share such devastating news with them."

"Horrible that they should be going through this, they clearly loved their son. What now? Visit the girlfriend?"

"If we can find her."

"Want me to see if Joanna can work her magic for us?"

"Yes, ring the station and, in the meantime, while we're on the doorstep, we might as well drop by the practice."

Lorne made the call, and Joanna promised to get back to her within the next half an hour. Sally looked up the address for the dentist and input the postcode in the satnav. Then drove the ten minutes to the location.

The receptionist welcomed them. Sally explained who they were and what they were doing there. She left her desk and returned with the practice manager who gave them the all-clear to take a copy of the files with them, which was a relief. It wasn't always that simple to obtain the vital information they needed to identify a victim.

Sally then decided to pick up some lunch for the team at the baker's on the corner. Once they were back in the car and en route to the station, Joanna rang and gave them the address for Vanessa Kitten.

"Thanks, Joanna, we'll stop off and see what she has to say then head back. I've already picked up some lunch for you guys."

"That's kind of you, boss, I'll let the others know. Good luck."

"Thanks. Just in case she's out, can you go through her socials for us? See if there is any information on her Facebook profile that tells us where she works."

"Hold the line, I can get that information for you now." There was a slight pause as Joanna pounded her keyboard. "Yes, here it is. She works at a blinds shop in Acle."

"Interesting, okay, we'll check if she's at home first. If there's no luck there, we'll head back to see if she's at work. What's the name of the shop?"

"Sunshine Blinds."

The address Joanna gave them was in Brundall, a small, terraced house, presumably a different type of property to the one she had shared with Dan, judging by what his parents had told them. Sally rang the bell. It was answered by a man in his thirties whose frame filled the doorway. He wore a T-shirt which showed off the size of his pecs as well as his bulging biceps. Sally smiled and flashed her warrant card at him.

"Hi, I'm DI Sally Parker, and this is my partner, DS Lorne Warner. We're here to see Vanessa Kitten. Does she still live here?"

"She does. Why? Has she done something illegal?" His eyes narrowed, and he looked Sally up and down from head to toe, lingering on her breasts before he switched his gaze to Lorne.

"No, we're hoping she can help us with our enquiries."

"About what?"

"That's a personal matter. Is she in or not?"

He crossed his arms and rippled his tanned, oversized biceps for effect. "Not. Is that it?"

"Not quite. Is she at work?"

"Yep. Don't ask me where that is, I ain't gonna tell you."

"Is there a reason for that?"

"Because I don't talk to your mob. Filth by name, filth by nature in my experience."

"Sorry if you've been treated badly by my colleagues in the past."

"Whatever. You're all the same. Try to fit people up just to suit yourselves, mainly when they're innocent. Just because I choose to take care of myself down at the gym, it doesn't mean I'm a thug."

"I only have your word for that. What time does her shift finish?"

"Pass, ask me another."

"What time does she usually get home in the evening? Sorry, I didn't catch your name, what is it?"

"Carl Spencer, and I have no idea. I'm always down the gym from six, and yes, that's every evening. You don't get a physique like this from missing every other night lifting weights."

"I can imagine. Okay, thanks for your time. We'll catch her at work then. Enjoy the rest of your day."

"Oh, I will." He slammed the door in their faces.

"Rude man," Sally cursed under her breath as they turned and walked back to the car.

"I wouldn't go saying that to his face in a hurry." Lorne chuckled.

"All brawn and no brains, that's usually the case with his sort, isn't it?"

"Again, not something I'd have the courage to say to his face."

Sally nudged her in the side. "Coward."

"Yep, I am. Gone are the days I pick fights with his type. Back in the day, when I was a feisty Met cop, well, that would have been a different story."

It was Sally's turn to laugh. She slipped into the driver's seat and said, "I know, your reputation was second to none. No one messed with the great Lorne Simpkins, not if they wanted to hang on to their limbs."

"You're too funny. It was a different way of life back then. There are far too many restrictions on what we can and can't do with a suspect these days."

"There is that, which is why we're part of the Cold Case Team, although even that can test us at times, can't it?"

"It can."

Sally started the engine and drove back to Acle. Lorne pulled up the postcode for the blinds shop, and it turned out to be a couple of streets from the dentist's. "Ever feel like you're going round in circles?"

"Often, it goes with the territory, doesn't it?"

They both laughed.

FIVE MINUTES LATER, they entered the showroom of the blinds company and asked the female assistant if they could speak with the manager. She sauntered off and returned with a young man in his mid-twenties in tow.

"Hello, I'm Mr Coombes, how can I help you?"

Sally and Lorne flashed their IDs.

"Sorry to show up unannounced, we were in the area. Is it possible to speak with Vanessa Kitten, please?"

"Umm... this is highly unusual. May I ask what this is about?"

"It's a personal matter. Can we speak to her?"

"No, not on my time. It's inconvenient at this time, she's

in the packing room, we have an important order to get ready for delivery."

"I quite understand, but it really wouldn't take long."

He peeked at his watch. Sally did the same. By this time the morning had flown by and the afternoon had begun.

"It's twelve-thirty, she's due to have a lunch break in half an hour. I won't have any objection to you speaking with her then, although she might." He smirked.

Sally had to suppress her anger. She took an instant dislike to this man. I thought he was the type to shove it down his staff's throats to let them know he was in charge and what he said went. "We don't mind waiting. If you can ask her to join us outside, we're parked at the front."

"I'll do that. Goodbye." He turned on his heel and went through the same door from which he'd appeared moments earlier.

"Jumped-up prick, who the fuck does he think he is?" Sally muttered on their way back out to the car.

"Keep smiling, you can have a rant outside, he's probably got this place rigged up with cameras."

"You reckon? What a tosser. There are plenty more names I'd like to call him as well."

"But you're not going to." Lorne sniggered.

They left the showroom and walked back to the car.

"We could eat our lunch while we're waiting, that is, if you're not too worked up about him."

Sally shrugged. "We might as well. Some people really tick me off without even trying, especially these days. Why is that?"

Lorne dipped her hand into the bag of sandwiches and passed Sally her tuna mayo on brown. "Because you let them wind you up. It's your biggest flaw."

Sally whipped her head around to face her partner. "What? Are you saying I have more than one flaw?"

Lorne winced. "Maybe that came out wrong, sorry, and it's not just you. Ouch, you're going to despise me after what I have to say."

"Go on, don't be shy, the damage has already been done."

"Oh heck. All I was trying to say is that it's natural for our patience to wane as we get older, and wiser, of course."

Sally chuckled. "Nice swerve. I think that's definitely true. Especially in his case, jumped-up little fucker. Eat up, I refuse to let a dickhead like that spoil my lunch."

"That's the ticket."

They managed to eat three-quarters of their sandwich by the time a young woman in jeans and trainers came out from a side door of the building. Sally shoved her sandwich in Lorne's lap and exited the car.

"Hi, are you Vanessa Kitten?"

The woman's eyes narrowed, and she walked towards the car. "I am. My boss told me you wanted to see me. I don't know why, I haven't done anything wrong."

"We know that. Why don't we have a chat in the car?"

"I can only spare you ten minutes. A girl has to eat, and my tyrant of a boss only gives us half an hour for lunch. He makes us work over if we're a minute late back, too."

"Don't worry, we won't keep you too long, I promise."

Sally opened the back door for Vanessa, and she eased into the back seat.

"We've got an extra sandwich, if you want one?"

"No thanks, I'm on a diet and have cut out all types of bread."

"Ah, okay. No problem."

"Can we get on with this? I want to know why the police would show up at my work and cause this much embarrassment for me."

Sally twisted in her seat to view the woman properly, eager to see what her reaction would be once she shared the news. "We're truly sorry about that. We're dealing with an investigation, and your name came up during our enquiries."

"What? I swear, I ain't done nothing wrong. Christ, my father would kill me if I did, he's a real stickler for doing the right thing."

"Sorry, maybe I misled you there. I'm going to come to the point."

"I wish you would."

"Have you seen the news in the last few days?"

"I don't watch the news, it's too depressing. Life is bad enough as it is right now. And don't even start on the cost-of-living crisis or politics. I think everyone has had their fill of that crap this year, haven't they?"

"You're not wrong. I was referring more to the local news rather than the main news bulletins?"

"Nope, it's still depressing. Why? Have I missed something important?"

Sally nodded. "A couple of days ago we were called out to Wayland Wood, do you know it?"

"Everyone in the area knows it, why?"

"Because a body had been discovered."

Vanessa gasped. "How awful. It's beautiful around there. But what does that have to do with me?"

"We believe the victim is Dan Jessop."

Vanessa's eyes widened, and her breathing came in fits and starts. Her hand covered her chest, and she whispered, "This can't be true... not after all this time. Are you sure it's him?"

"We're almost certain. He was wearing the watch his parents gave him."

"Oh shit! I didn't think it would end like this."

Sally and Lorne exchanged concerned glances.

"Like what?" Sally probed.

"Well, he went missing, dropped me in all kinds of shit

financially two years ago. He just disappeared, and now you're telling me he's dead. Where has he been all that time? Why didn't he contact me?"

"All good questions that we're eager to learn the answers to. Perhaps you can tell us what happened around the time he went missing?"

"God, I can't remember now. That proves it wasn't that important, doesn't it? When my brain refuses to recall what happened."

"Some people prefer to block out bad incidences, is that the case here?"

She sighed and shook her head. "You're asking me something I can't really answer. All I know is that I loved him and, all of a sudden, he chose to walk away from me. I had to give up the beautiful home we shared because I didn't have the money coming in to cover all the bills."

"If you can try and think back, maybe to the days just before he went missing."

She closed her eyes. "I can try. Yes, we went out for dinner the day before he went missing."

"That's great, what else can you remember?"

"We were happy, most of the time. Dan was generous with his money but occasionally lashed out when things didn't go his way."

Sally sidestepped the obvious question for a moment or two. "He was a property developer, wasn't he?"

"That's right. He was good at it, too, that's how we came to live in our house. He had to take out a small mortgage, I think it was about a hundred grand or so, which is tiny compared to what some of my friends have around their necks today. It's eye-watering what people owe, just to own a home these days. It's getting harder and harder to get on the ladder, and the government couldn't give a toss."

"Do you rent now?"

"Yes, I could never afford to own a house. Everything is so expensive compared to when my parents were younger."

"Times were different back then. I bet they struggled in their day, because the wages were that much lower compared to what they are now."

"I suppose you're right. I've never really thought about it in those terms before. There's only one winner today, the banks, right?"

Sally smiled. "Yep. So, Dan bought and renovated properties and did well out of it. Did you have a say in the business?"

"*No way.* It was all down to him, he never asked me for my opinion about anything."

"That's a shame. Did that cause a rift between you?"

She closed her eyes again, and her chin dropped to her chest. "Sometimes," she mumbled.

"Did you have a happy relationship, or was it fraught at times?"

She raised her head to stare at Sally. "We argued, name me a couple who don't. Having money in his pocket changed him, and not for the better either."

"Did he abuse you?" Sally asked the one question she'd been longing to ask.

Vanessa chewed on her fingernails for a few seconds and nodded. "Once or twice. He was always sorry when he hit me. Oh God, just admitting that out loud brings back so may dreadful memories. I honestly thought I had successfully blocked them out, I guess I was wrong. I loved him, I thought it was the norm at the time for blokes to talk with their fists. I know differently now, of course."

"Meaning?"

"Carl never hits out. He might come across as a real bruiser but he's a gentleman once you get to know him. A genuine softie inside."

"How long have you been together?"

She covered her eyes with her right hand. "I hate to admit this, but I started seeing him on the side a month before Dan went missing. Please, don't think badly of me."

"Don't be silly, of course we won't. Were you intending to finish with Dan?"

"Yes, I was waiting for the right time to come my way."

"Did Carl know you were in a relationship at the time you started seeing him?"

"No, I kept it from him. I'm not a horrible person, I promise. Life with Dan was up and down, not that his parents ever saw that side of him. They always thought he was a saint. I didn't have the heart to put them right. Have you seen them?"

"Yes, Dan's mother rang the station this morning to tell me that she believed the watch belonged to her son."

"I'm confused. How did she know about the watch?"

"I put out a press conference at the beginning of the week, and her friend saw it. Mr and Mrs Jessop were away at the time."

"Ah, I see now. They never really liked me. She cornered me one day, told me that she didn't think I was good enough for her son. I was mortified, I'd done everything I could to be nice to her up until then. After that conversation, I began to take a closer look at my relationship with Dan, and to be honest, I quickly came to the conclusion, that it was nothing but a sham." She fell silent, and her eyes narrowed as if she had remembered something important.

"Has something else come back to you, Vanessa?"

"You could say that. We were having a meal the week before he went missing. I wasn't a great cook, but what I served up was always edible. Anyway, that night I had cooked a casserole. According to him it lacked any kind of flavour—it didn't. I hate eating the food I make, but that meal was really tasty, so I knew he was talking nonsense. I got the impression he was trying to provoke me, to initiate an argument. I walked away from the table and started clearing up. He came up behind me, pinned me to the sink, ran the hot water then stuck my arm under the tap." She raised the sleeve of her jacket. "It's still noticeable today. He did that and for no damn reason."

"I'm sorry you went through that. Was anyone else aware of the abuse?"

"No, I was a fool, I tried to ignore the signs, pretended it wasn't happening to me. I loved him, well, in the beginning. Carl was my saviour in more ways than one. He gave me the courage to stand up for myself. The next time Dan tried to abuse me I pulled a knife on him. He broke down, realised how much the money had changed him and begged for my forgiveness. At first, I believed him, but he turned out to be a manipulative bastard. He caught me off guard and pretended he wanted to make it up to me in the bedroom. I'm sure I don't need to go into details there."

"What happened?"

"He took a swipe at me, caught me on the jaw. I fell to the floor, unconscious. When I woke up a little while later, he had tied my wrists to the bed. I couldn't believe it. He got on top of me. I tried to kick out, but he got wise to what I was up to and sat on my legs. Forced me against my will to have sex with him. I said I didn't want to, and he told me either I spread my legs for him or he would pay my sister a visit and…"

"Oh no, that's despicable. Why didn't you tell anyone about it?"

"I couldn't, I felt too ashamed. This is the first time I've said it out loud. I felt so dirty after he did that to me. I knew then that I had to get away from him, I just didn't know how."

"Is that when you started seeing Carl?"

"No, I started seeing him a couple of weeks after Dan raped me. I decided to join the local gym, thought it was important for me to enrol in a self-defence class they were running at the time. I went along by myself. I told Dan I was going to an evening class at the college. He didn't ask what it was for, he just accepted it. I met Carl the first night. He caught my eye, and we ended up leaving the gym at the same time after our sessions had ended. He asked me to go for a drink with him. I didn't see any harm in it at the time. He turned out to be the complete opposite to Dan. He was attentive, listened to what I had to say instead of cutting me off mid-sentence, the way Dan did. I soon found out I had more in common with Carl than Dan. I know that probably sounds awful, but I have no regrets."

"It doesn't. We're not here to cast aspersions, all we're after are the facts. Are you sure Carl didn't know about Dan when you started seeing him?"

"No, he didn't. I only met up with him while I was at the gym to begin with. He was the perfect gentleman, treated me with respect, something that Dan used to do at the beginning of our relationship. That all went to pot once I moved in with him. He tried to control me, told me what clothes I should be wearing and what friends I should be seeing. I saw it as him protecting me at first, until he burnt my arm and tied me to the bed then threatened me with my sister."

"How did you get out of the situation?"

"I didn't, not really. I was constantly thinking about how I could get away from him, and then all of a sudden, he went missing. That's when the confusion set in. I didn't know what to do for the best. I stopped going to the gym, more out of guilt than anything else. I didn't see Carl again for a few months after Dan went missing. I finished work and went looking for him every night. I still loved him. It's probably hard for you to get your heads around that. It took me a while to realise he wasn't coming back."

"Did he pack a case or just disappear?"

"One minute he was there, the next he was gone. I checked his wardrobe, and nothing seemed to be missing, including his bag. To be honest with you, I wasn't sure what to think. I rang his parents; they're the ones who reported him missing. My mind was all over the place at the time. They swept in and took control of the situation. I kind of went into my shell and struggled to get out of it. I lost my job. I worked in a department store at the time, and then everything overwhelmed me. I had no idea how I was going to cover the bills or the mortgage. Dan's phone was dead… I had no way of contacting him. I remember thinking this was him playing mind games with me, but as the days stretched into weeks and then months, I began to think he was never going to come back. Then the blasted bailiffs turned up. He'd taken out a credit card in my name that I didn't know existed."

"Hold on, were his parents aware of this?"

"No, I kept it from them. They showed up when the bailiffs were on my doorstep and offered to pay the debt off for me. Once the men left, the Jessops read me the riot act and ordered me to pack my bags. I didn't put up a fight because I didn't have it in me. I was under the doctor for depression, another fact they weren't aware of. I felt so alone, and here they were, ordering me to leave the house I loved."

Sally reached between the seats and placed her hand over Vanessa's. "I'm so sorry, you didn't deserve to be treated like that when you were at your lowest ebb."

"Thank you. I'm thankful I didn't crumble and was able to get on with my life. I slept on a friend's sofa for a week or two, until I outstayed my welcome and began going to the gym again; my doctor advised me it would be good for my mental health. That's when Carl and I met up again. He still has no idea of the trauma I'd been through. He thinks I got into debt and had to sell up."

"Why did you decide not to tell him?"

"I guess because I didn't want him to feel sorry for me. Let's face it, I didn't have all the answers to have that discussion with anyone."

"I can understand that. Did you ever hear from Dan again? Sense him around, perhaps watching you?"

Vanessa shuddered at the thought. "Gosh, no. I just thought he'd moved on. The police didn't want to know, I presumed they thought the same."

"I'm sorry our colleagues let the family down, that was wrong of them."

"It didn't bother me. Deep down I was glad he left me, even if it didn't make sense at the time."

"Do you know if he'd had any problems with his business?"

"No, definitely not. Everything was going full steam ahead in that respect. He'd recently sold his latest property. I seem to remember he was on the lookout for a new one; the auction house rang him the day before he went missing. They always kept him in the loop when there were lots he might be interested in. Strange how the shutters have gone up in my mind now and I'm able to remember everything."

"The brain can be a complex organ. What else can you tell us? His parents mentioned that he had a builder working alongside him, can you tell us more about him?"

"Blimey, I'm not sure, I only met him once or twice when he called at the house with an issue he needed to resolve the following day with one of the properties. What the hell was his name?"

"It would be really helpful if you could remember."

"I'm doing my very best. Robin something, yes, I'm sure it was. Maybe his parents will be able to help you out."

"It's okay, we'll get in touch with them later. I take it the builder was local?"

"Yes, although I'm not quite sure where he lived. Sorry, that's not very helpful to you."

"Don't worry, we have ways of sourcing information like that. Is there anything else you can tell us?"

"Not really, no. He pretty much kept me out of his business, told me that I wouldn't be able to understand the complexities… if that's the right word for it?"

"It is. You've been open and fair with us. I repeat, I'm sorry you had to go through that experience."

"It's in the past now. I'm not denying it took me a while to get over it. But it's all good in the end. I'm with Carl, he always treats me well. That's all we girls want in the end, isn't it? To know we're loved and in safe hands with our partners."

"That's true and the way all relationships should be. Thanks for taking the time out of your day to speak with us. I'll give you one of my cards. If you think of anything else you want to add, give me a call."

"Thank you. Can you answer a question for me?"

"I'll try," Sally replied.

"Why has it taken two years for his body to surface?"

"That's something we can't really answer right now."

"Oh God, did a dog dig him up, is that it? Was his body buried in the woods?"

Sally sighed. "No, that wasn't the case at all. Okay, I'm going to tell you, but this mustn't go any further. The pathologist believes that Dan's body was frozen."

"What? Oh my Lord, you're kidding me?"

"Sadly not. We can't tell you when he was frozen."

"Oh my God, that's awful, truly terrible. His poor parents. How did they take the news?"

"Better than expected. They've asked to view his body this afternoon."

"Oh shit! Rather them than me. I couldn't do that, not if you paid me several million pounds. I had to see my grandmother lying in her coffin before she was buried, and that image still haunts me every night. It's something I never want to experience again, not even with my own parents. I think it's better to remember them as they were, not when their souls have left them."

"I believe I'm inclined to think the same. Thanks again for being so open with us."

"You're welcome. I know I haven't given you much, but I hope it helps in some small way. Though Dan had his faults, he still didn't deserve to die at such a young age, no one does."

"The world is an unfair place to live in sometimes, that's for sure. Take care of yourself, Vanessa."

"Thank you, I will. I have a good man beside me."

"Glad to hear it."

Vanessa smiled and left the car.

"Well, that was an eye-opener," Lorne stated once the back door had closed.

Sally stretched the knots out of her back, which had developed due to the awkward position she'd been in during the interview, and started the engine. "Wasn't it just? I'm not sure what to think of it yet. I'm going to need to take time to process everything she's told us. I think the first step is for us to find the builder Dan employed to carry out the renovations."

Lorne removed the mobile from her pocket and began the search. "I'll see what I can find en route."

"Whether you manage to find him or not, we should get back to the station and deliver the team their lunch before it gets too late."

Lorne nodded, committed to her search. Sally drew away from the kerb. Out of the corner of her eye, she saw Coombes staring out of the window at her. "Tosser."

"Leave it, don't let him get to you," Lorne warned.

Sally turned and flashed Coombes one of her warmest smiles and through gritted teeth said, "I hope our paths cross again soon, arsehole."

CHAPTER 3

During the afternoon, the team managed to locate the builder who had worked with Dan. Sally arranged for Lorne and herself to drop in on him, on the way home, after their shift. As soon as Sally laid eyes on him, she had him nailed as a decent chap.

Robin Askew pulled up outside his large, detached home situated on the edge of Mulbarton, a village just over fifteen minutes from Brundall, where Dan had lived.

"Nice place, at least from the front," Lorne said. "Builders tend to keep all their crap in the back garden, though, don't they?"

"Which is one thing I will never understand. It's not a very good advert for their business, is it?"

"Because most builders know there is a shortage of tradesmen these days, they don't feel the need to bother about what their own property looks like."

"You're right. Okay, let's see what he can tell us, if anything. He sounded a touch guarded on the phone earlier."

They exited the vehicle at the same time as Askew hopped out of his van.

He gestured at the dirty clothes he was wearing. "Excuse the mess, I've been overseeing the laying of a concrete floor in someone's kitchen today. I had to jump in and rescue a tool from the mix before the final level was... nope, I can tell by your expressions that's not the kind of information you want to hear."

Sally laughed. "Don't take it personally. We have a tendency to switch off when our husbands are together, discussing their work. They run a property development business together."

"Ah, gotcha. Do they do well?"

"Yes, it was touch and go for a while during the pandemic, what with the price of the materials seemingly going up weekly, but now that they're more settled, things appear to be looking up. Thanks for sparing the time to meet up with us this evening, we really appreciate it."

"It's my pleasure, not that I'm going to be able to tell you much about Dan. I've had time to mull over a few things during this afternoon's activities and haven't come up with anything that I think will prove helpful to you. Come inside. You'll have to excuse the mess in there as well, my thirteen-year-old daughter has just twisted my arm into getting her a puppy. We're in the process of toilet training it at the moment."

"Lorne's the lady you should be speaking to about that. She runs a rescue kennel on the side." Sally faced Lorne who rolled her eyes as her cheeks coloured up.

"Really? Wow, how the heck do you pull that one off? I thought being a copper would be enough to keep you busy during the day."

"It is. I employ a manager to run the kennels on a daily basis and I take over in the evening. I have the best end of the deal." Lorne laughed. "Have you bought any pads for the pup to use?"

"Yes, we didn't have any at first, but my daughter looked up online what to get the pooch to help make the transition easier for it. Tommy, that's the pup, came from a reputable breeder about ten minutes up the road. She gave us a few tips, but we must be doing something wrong because every day I come home to either my wife or my daughter cursing at the poor thing."

"What breed is it?" Lorne asked.

"It's a mixed breed. In my day they were called mongrels, these days they've got fancy names which cost a packet. Let me think, it's either a Cockerpoo or a Labradoodle, I can't for the life of me remember."

"Is it small or large?"

"Tiny at the moment, so I haven't got a clue what size it's going to be when it grows up. You'll see for yourself." He led the way through the front garden. Shouting erupted as soon as he slipped his key in the front door. "Shit, here we go again. Every night for the past week has been the same."

"Maybe Lorne can give your wife and daughter some pointers while we have a chat?"

"I'd love that, would you?" Robin asked, his anxiety evident.

"I'll give it a try. It's been a while since I've had to deal with a puppy, but it can't hurt to give your family a few basic tips, if they're willing to listen, that is."

"They will, we will, we're desperate to find a solution. I don't think people realise how much hard work is involved owning a puppy."

"It's definitely underestimated, that's why so many dogs end up at rescue centres, because the dogs grow out of the puppy stage and people can't be bothered to put in the hours of training. They can be worse than children sometimes. Sorry, I'll get off my soapbox now."

"Maria, we have visitors," Robin bellowed.

A blonde woman carrying a spray bottle and cloth appeared at the end of the hallway. Her hair was mostly tied back, but tendrils had escaped on either side, framing her ruddy face. "You'll have to excuse the smell. I've done my best to get rid of it. Tommy doesn't care where he poops at the moment."

"Ah, we have an expert in our midst. This officer, sorry, I didn't catch your name."

"It's Lorne. Hi."

"Lorne runs a rescue kennel. She's offered to give us a few pointers if you're open to it, love."

"Christ yes. I'm going to snap your hand off after hearing that suggestion."

Lorne smiled and walked up the hallway to deal with the puppy issue. Robin led Sally into his study across the hallway from the front door.

"Oops, I truly thought this room was tidier than the rest of the house."

"Don't worry, as long as there is a place for me to sit and take notes, that's all I'm concerned about."

"Yes, here you go. Let's sweep this pile up and put it on the floor. I'm sure I'll get around to sorting out my paperwork soon." He peered over his shoulder. "My wife used to handle the admin work for me, but now all her time has been taken up caring for the new arrival. I wouldn't be exaggerating if I said we're all overwhelmed, especially Maria."

Sally sat in the now clutter-free chair and removed her notebook from her pocket. "I know I was a tad vague over the phone; thanks again for allowing us to come by this evening."

"I was intrigued by your call. You mentioned your enquiries were concerning Dan Jessop. How can I help? Bearing in mind I haven't seen him for a couple of years."

"I completely understand. I have to tell you that Dan's body was discovered at the beginning of the week."

Robin tutted, ran a hand through his curly dark hair and rested his backside on the edge of his messy desk. "I had a feeling this would be the result one day."

Sally inclined her head and asked, "What makes you say that?"

He shrugged. "Because the guy has been missing for over two years. We were pretty close before he disappeared."

"Close? As in he discussed his personal life with you, or was your relationship a purely professional one?"

"A mixture of both, if you like. I didn't really want to know the ins and outs of his relationship with his girlfriend. I never liked her. On the odd occasion I met her there always seemed to be something wrong about her, don't ask me to go into detail, I'd have trouble putting my finger on it. I come across all types of people in my line of business, and to say she was… I suppose 'full of herself' would be close to the mark."

Having met Vanessa earlier, Sally struggled to understand what he was getting at. "Are you aware of what their relationship was like?"

"No, like I've said already, I prefer to keep out of people's relationships, it doesn't work sticking your nose in where it's not wanted. One of my lads, a brickie, he told me he saw her down at his local gym, flirting with a muscle-bound goon, not once but several times."

"I understand. We interviewed her earlier, and she was open with us about her relationship."

His eyebrow rose. "Do you mean she was having an affair with this fella?"

Sally nodded. "It seems that way. Do you know if Dan knew about it?"

"God, poor bloke. I mean, she's nothing special to look at, is she?"

"I can't possibly comment," Sally swerved the question. She'd found Vanessa to be anything but plain, but she wouldn't have called her beautiful either. "Did Dan know?" she asked again.

"If you're pushing me for an answer, I would have to say I believe he had an inkling, but he didn't come right out and tell me."

"Could there have been something else bothering him?"

"Who knows? He didn't confide in me, which was a blessing in disguise. I have enough shit of my own to deal with having a teenager in the house and running my business. I'd rather not get involved in people's personal lives. He was an associate, there was a line drawn that neither of us crossed to make sure things remained professional between us."

Sally nodded. "Okay, I get that. I'm just trying to find clues or evidence to assist our investigation. I assumed you might be able to shed some light on the day-to-day running of his business."

He shrugged a second time. "He employed me as a contractor, I had no reason to butt my nose into what he did with the properties. He told me what to do on site, yes, if I felt his ideas were off the mark I told him, but other than that I went along with his instructions and so did my men. Can you tell me what happened to Dan?"

"Not really. His body was discovered in Wayland Wood on Monday. We haven't got a clue how he got there. We're assuming someone dumped his body."

"Are you telling me someone has held him hostage all this time? I thought it was weird, him going missing like that. One day we were making arrangements to go to an auction together, the next, there was nothing. I tried calling him, but his phone went straight to voicemail."

"So, he'd contacted you the day before, is that it?"

"I think so, as far as I can remember. It was all very strange at the time. I went to his house that night, and his girlfriend told me she hadn't seen him and slammed the door in my face. I thought that was uncalled for back then, in fact, I still do. There's something off about her. Are you sure you didn't pick up on it when you interviewed her?"

"No, I didn't sense she was hiding anything at all, quite the opposite. She was open and honest, as far as I could tell."

"Really? Do you usually take someone's word on what goes on when you challenge them during an interview?"

"Not always. As coppers we know what questions to ask at the right time. When I delved into what had happened around Dan's disappearance, I got the impression she was telling the truth."

"And are your instincts ever wrong, Inspector?"

"Not usually, but if you feel there's a need for us to dig further then I'll take that on board."

"Don't forget she had this bodybuilder on the side, up to all sorts with him, no doubt."

"Thanks, we'll do some extra digging on both of them. While you were on site at any of the properties he renovated, did you ever see anyone hanging around outside, up to no good?"

"I don't think so. Mind you, you're expecting me to recall things that might have happened a couple of years ago, and like most men, I couldn't possibly tell you what I had for dinner at the weekend."

Sally smiled. "Fair enough. I'm sure you can understand how frustrating all of this is for us. All we're trying to ascertain is how and why Dan disappeared and where he's been in the two years since then."

"Yep, I've said it numerous times over the years, I wouldn't like to be a copper, not when the criminals appear to be getting craftier these days at a time when there seems to be fewer police patrolling our streets."

"It's getting harder and harder to police the country, but then, I believe that can be said about every job or career these days. I bet things have changed considerably since you served your apprenticeship in the building trade, haven't they?"

He nodded. "I have to admit, you're spot on about that. The whole world has turned upside down in the last twenty years or so, at least that's the way it seems most days. The tradesmen are few and far between. I have to employ guys who have all-round skills, just in case I can't get a true tradesman to take on a job. It was never like that when I started out. My father would be turning in his grave if he saw the state of the building trade right now. And don't get me started about the youth of today, they're not interested in doing the basic training, they'd much rather be sat at home on their PlayStations than ending up covered in shit such as what I had to deal with today. God help anyone wanting to employ a builder in twenty or thirty years, the costs will be through the roof because of the lack of tradesmen available. Bugger, sorry for the rant, I knew I wouldn't be able to stop once I got started. Hey, I hope your other half has got a decent crew he can rely on? I bet he's forking out good money for them, if he has."

"Thankfully, he has. I totally understand what you're saying about the youth of today. From what I've been told, the Force is struggling to recruit youngsters, as well, so I suppose that can be said about any career. I fear for this country going forward. We've been too reliant on immigrants for too many years, and now... nope, I'm not going there. I try to avoid discussing politics wherever possible."

"I'm with you on that. Only last week I had to visit the job centre. I put up a vacancy for a bricklayer. I noticed there were six other adverts on the board wanting a brickie. It made me check out the rest of the vacancies ready to be filled. There are dozens of jobs available, however, people are averse to getting their hands dirty."

"I think we could discuss this topic for hours, but where would it get us in the end?"

"You're probably right. Still good to have a decent whinge now and again."

Lorne appeared in the doorway.

"How did you get on?" Sally asked.

"I'm in love. Tommy is such a sweetheart. I've given your wife and daughter a link to a website I refer to constantly when other dog owners have any issues. Your pup, just like a baby, needs to have a routine."

"Don't we all?" Robin joked. "Don't worry, we'll do everything to ensure he settles down soon. We all love him. I'm looking forward to the day I get lumbered with taking him for a walk. It might give me an hour's peace in the evening."

Lorne and Sally both smirked.

"We both love our dogs. They don't ask for much in the grand scheme of things and they're not with us that long either, sadly."

"I know, it's heartbreaking. I always had dogs when I was growing up, but this is the first time we've taken on a puppy, and that's only because my daughter wouldn't give me a break. We waited until she was thirteen and then started our search. We were lucky to get Tommy. My friend was supposed to have him, but his wife was diagnosed with breast cancer, and they felt they wouldn't be able to devote the time needed to raise a pup. I felt sorry for them and offered to take Tommy on. He's a little character, full of mischief."

"Most pups of his age are," Lorne said. "I'm sure he'll turn out to be a great addition to your family. I've given your wife my card. Don't hesitate to ring me if you need any further advice. It would be better to get in touch in the evening, you know, what with the day job being so important."

"I bet. Thanks again. Is there anything else I can help you with regarding Dan?"

"I think we've covered it all now. If you can add anything in the future, don't hesitate to give me a ring." Sally gave him one of her cards and rose from her seat.

"I'm sorry I couldn't tell you much, hopefully what I have told you will come in handy during the investigation. I'll show you out."

They followed him to the front door.

"We'll be in touch if we need to ask any further questions. It was a pleasure meeting you."

"Hey, maybe I should give you one of my business cards, in case your hubby needs a hand in the future."

"Of course, it's always good to have a backup plan in place. None of us know what's awaiting us around the next corner."

"Ain't that the truth? Goodnight, ladies."

On the way back to the car, Sally asked, "How did you really get on back there?"

"I had to bite my tongue when I first walked into the kitchen."

"Oh God, why? Or shouldn't I ask? They weren't ill-treating the dog, were they?"

Lorne grimaced. "They were. I tried to keep my temper in check. I took the pup from the mother; it was petrified and clung to me when I cuddled it. I then tried to tell them they were doing things all wrong. That's when Maria broke down and admitted she was finding it hard to cope with the demands of the pup and the accidents were getting on her nerves. She complained about spending hours each day cleaning carpets."

"What did they expect? Some people make me sick. They envisage taking on a dog or puppy that is fully trained, which is nonsense. How did you leave it with them? Thank goodness we called round to see them before things escalated."

"I know, it breaks my heart to think how that ten-week-old pup has been treated since they got him. No dog deserves that. I doubt if it's been shown any kind of love since they brought it home."

Sally stopped mid-stride. "Oh no, don't say that. I want to go back and rescue it."

"No, leave it for now. I had a serious talk with both of them, and they've promised to ring me if they get overwhelmed with it all."

"Do you trust them to do the right thing?"

"I'm not sure. We'll have to wait and see."

Sally opened the driver's door and got in. "If you don't mind me saying so, you don't seem that concerned, Lorne."

"Oh, believe me, I am, however, I've learnt to switch off the emotional side and consider the practicalities of a situation before I judge someone. More often than not, it's people's ignorance which is in question in animal abuse cases. I'll check back in with them in a day or two, after they've had a chance to look up the website I gave them the link to. It covers all the basics from bringing the puppy home to introducing them to the vet for their inoculations, to being a responsible owner and having them spayed or neutered once they're old enough."

"And what was their reaction to you showing them where they were going wrong?"

"They accepted it, at least they appeared to. Only time will tell, eh?"

Sally sighed and drove them home. "It's been a long day. I'm undecided if it has been productive or not."

"What makes you say that?"

"The conversation I had with Robin. He's just made me doubt whether the lovely Vanessa was telling us the truth or not."

"Huh? What did he say?"

Sally recounted what the builder had told her.

"Crikey, so what are you saying? That Vanessa should be sitting at the top of our suspect list?"

"I'm thinking both of them, Vanessa and Carl, should be right up there. That needs to be our main priority tomorrow, to check out their backgrounds. See if anything dodgy shows up. If what we saw was all an act earlier, then I have to doubt my role as a police officer going forward."

"Don't be so ridiculous. If, and it's a huge *if*, she's told us a pack of lies, then she fooled me as much as you. I can't see it myself. You know we both work on what our gut instinct tells us. I have to say, the alarm bells weren't going ten to the dozen while we were interviewing her. Yes, I think we should carry out due diligence on them as a matter of caution but, like you, I don't feel apprehensive or duped in the slightest by what she told us."

Sally nodded. "Thanks, Lorne. In that case, we can't both be wrong, can we?"

"Nope. And I wouldn't go losing sleep over it either. I know how something like this has affected you in the past."

"I'm good, don't worry about me. Shit, what about the doctor's appointment for Tony?"

"I rang him earlier, told him we were snowed under interviewing people and he assured me he wouldn't miss the appointment."

"Sorry, mate, you should have been there with him."

"If I can't trust him to tell the doctor what's wrong with

his wound then I might as well say goodbye to my marriage now. I'm sure everything will be fine."

"Let me know later how he got on, if you get five minutes alone."

"I will, I promise."

Lorne fell silent after that. Sally decided to end the conversation there. Instead, her mind worked overtime, going over different scenarios for the victim's demise, but nothing really stood out to her. One thing she contemplated and dismissed right away was Vanessa and her boyfriend's involvement, more to do with the length of time Dan was held before his body was eventually dumped. Where would they have held him all that time for a start? And there was also the fact that Vanessa had been very open with them during the interview, unless that was a ploy to put them off the scent, which she doubted.

CHAPTER 4

"So, the doctor has told him to basically take more care of himself, is that it?" Sally asked the second Lorne got in the car the following morning.

"That's it in a nutshell. He's been that tired lately, and I don't want this to sound awful, he hasn't really been caring for his wound as well as he should have been at the end of the day. He should be showering in the evening, but he's been too tired to do that. The risks of infection are obviously greater when he neglects to take the proper precautions to avoid it."

"I get that. Do you want me to have a word with Simon? Maybe get him to cut down Tony's hours slightly? I can't imagine giving him the odd hour off here and there will hurt."

"No, I think we should leave it up to them to sort out. Needless to say, I read my old man the riot act last night."

Sally sniggered. "I would have loved to have been a fly on the wall during that conversation."

It was Lorne's turn to laugh. "I assure you, you wouldn't. All ended well, though."

Sally lifted a hand off the steering wheel. "I think we'll leave the conversation there before you go into detail."

"Cheeky, as if I would."

"How is Tony this morning?"

"He seemed to be in a good mood. He grabbed a shower before he went to bed last night, and I rubbed…"

"No, stop, that's too much information right there."

"Don't be such an idiot, I was about to say before we both rubbed the cream on his wound. I took a peek at it this morning while he was sleeping, and it didn't seem as red or angry, so that's a bonus."

"That's great. I'm glad you're on the case, I think things might have turned out badly if you hadn't forced him to go to the doctor's."

"Yep. Enough personal stuff. Knowing you, I bet you spent the evening going over all the information we gathered yesterday. Did you come to any conclusion?"

"Then you'd be wrong. I decided to set the case aside until we do the necessary digging on the couple today. I still don't think we have much to go on at this stage."

"I agree, but what else can we do? Unless something significant comes our way in the meantime, it might be a case of us revisiting Vanessa to question her further and bringing her fella in for an interview, get them rattled, and see what comes from that."

"You might be right. Yet another frustrating case for us to deal with, eh?"

"Is there any other type these days? Especially working the Cold Case Team."

"You're not meant to agree with me, you're supposed to assure me that new evidence will come our way soon that will have a positive impact on the investigation."

Lorne leaned forward and pointed to the sky. "And there's a huge pink sow passing overhead now."

Sally laughed. "You definitely missed your vocation. You should have been on the stage, Mrs Warner."

"Don't tempt me, it's not too late for me to retire from the Force again."

Sally shot a look at her partner. "You wouldn't dare!"

Lorne grinned. "You're right, I wouldn't."

Not long after, they arrived at the station, and Sally parked in her usual spot. They entered the station to find the desk sergeant, Pat Sullivan, trying to keep a man calm in the reception area.

Pat glanced up and caught Sally's eye. "Ah, here's the inspector now. Let me have a chat with her, see if she has time to see you."

"No, I have to go now. I can't do this, it was a mistake coming here."

Lorne instinctively took a step back towards the door, to block the man's exit if it was needed.

"Can I help at all?" Sally approached the counter and stood a few feet from the agitated man.

"Ah, yes, Inspector Parker. I believe this man has some news for you about the investigation you're dealing with at the moment."

"You do? I'd be interested in finding out more, sir. No pressure, a simple chat over a cup of tea or coffee will do. How does that sound to you?"

His hand flitted over his face, his agitation intensifying. Sally decided to give him some extra space.

"Come on, you've made it this far, why don't we have an informal chat? If things get too much for you, I won't hold it against you and you'll be free to go at any time during the interview, you have my word." She cringed, realising she'd gone from having a chat to mentioning an interview in the same sentence.

"Okay," the man shocked her by saying.

"Is the family room available at present, Sergeant?"

"It is, ma'am. I'll sort some drinks out for you all."

The man's eyes widened as the terror swept through him. "All? How many? Can't I just have a chat with you?"

Sally peered over her shoulder. "Just me and my partner, she'll be the one taking notes."

His gaze shot between Sally and Lorne, and he let out a relieved sigh, at least that's how Sally perceived it.

"Tea or coffee?" Sally asked.

"Tea, I don't drink coffee. All right, I'll speak to you."

Sally smiled. "Sugar and milk?"

"Three sugars, thanks, and yes, I'd like milk as well."

"You heard the man, Sergeant, one tea and two coffees, milk with one sugar for us."

"I'll bring them in."

Lorne remained by the exit until Sally had shown the man into the room off to the left that they used to have informal chats with members of the public.

He pulled out a chair and sat. Sally noted his chest was rising and falling rapidly and his hands were shaking until he clasped them together on the table in front of him.

Lorne joined them. She moved her chair closer to Sally, to ensure the man didn't feel intimidated if she sat near him. She flipped open her notebook to a clean page and poised her pen, ready to take down what he was hopefully going to tell them.

Sally's first question was interrupted by a knock on the door. She leapt out of her seat to answer it. Pat entered the room and placed a tray on the table then made a quick exit.

Sally handed the tea to the man and said, "Can we start by taking your name?"

"It's Kai Dawson, and yes, that's my real name."

"Is there any reason why I should doubt you?" Sally queried.

"No, everything I'm about to tell you is true."

"We're listening and intrigued as to what news you have for us."

He wrapped his hands around his cup and stared at the contents. "I'm not sure if I've done the right thing coming here today."

"Will you let us be the judge of that? What is it you want to tell us?"

He remained quiet for a few seconds and then whispered, "I saw them."

Lorne nudged Sally's leg under the table. "Saw who?"

"The body in the woods… I think I saw the two men who dumped it there."

"What? Can you describe these men?"

"One was shorter than the other, not by much, though. They were around six-foot-two, I suppose. Maybe I'm wrong about that, I was on my bike at the time."

"Did they see you?"

"Yes, that's why…"

"Why you've been worried about coming forward, is that it?" Sally finished his sentence for him.

"Worried? Scared shitless more like. Sorry for swearing."

"You don't have to apologise. Did the men say anything to you?"

"They seemed anxious about me being there. I didn't hang around, I pedalled fast to get out of there."

"Were you arriving or leaving the woods?"

"I had just got there, and they were on their way out of the woods."

"Did they say anything to you?" Sally repeated.

"No, nothing. The look was enough. I glanced over my

shoulder when I was about twenty feet from them, and they had both stopped and were staring at me. Put the wind up me, I can tell you. I usually take the same route back home, but I didn't that night because something didn't feel right about them."

"Did you see the body in the woods?"

"I don't think so. I saw the conference you put out the other day... I know I should have got in touch sooner, but I didn't know what the consequences would be."

"Why? You didn't do anything wrong."

"No, I know, but... it's hard, in case you haven't realised, I'm not a confident person. My head has been swimming for days, trying to make sense of it all. The last thing I want, or need, is to get caught up in something like this."

"There's really no need for you to be worried. Can you tell us anything else about the two men?"

"One was black and the other an older white male who appeared to be a bit scruffy."

Sally's intrigue piqued. "Scruffy, as in he might be homeless?"

"Oh no, sorry about that, I meant a labourer of sorts. He was wearing some kind of overalls, you know, with a bib and brace, that kind of thing, and they were covered in differently coloured paint, possibly a painter and decorator. Oh, I don't know, I might be wrong about that."

"That's a great piece of information, thank you. So, you were going in as they were coming out. I don't suppose you happened to see a vehicle in the car park, did you?"

"I've thought about this all week, and yes, there was a dark-coloured van in the car park."

"Any signage on the side, or did you see the number plate?"

"I caught part of it, not all of it. O-D-D, which I chuckled about at the time. And no, there was no signage. I think it was a black van, either that or a midnight blue. I didn't take that much notice of it, not really, except the letters on the number plate stood out. It's funny how certain items do that, isn't it?"

"It's amazing in some cases, this being one of them. It's surprising how important a tiny fact like that can turn out to be during an investigation. Is there anything else you can tell us about the men? Did they have short or long hair?"

"They both had short hair. It was starting to get dark by then. I know it's strange for me to go cycling through the woods at night. I have a lamp on my helmet that assists me. I don't go down there every night, just now and again. I find it challenging to ride in different locations at night."

"You're braver than me." Sally smiled. "What time did you arrive?"

"It was between ten and ten-fifteen."

"So, it would have been reasonably dark by then."

He nodded.

"How long do you ride for usually?"

"An hour in total, depends on the amount of stress I've had to deal with during the course of the day."

"What's your job?"

"I work as an accountant. Some days, since the pandemic, I work from home. That's when I take to the road. I hate being cooped up in the house."

"I can understand that. Is there anything else you can tell us?"

He glanced down at his half-drunk cup of tea and shook his head. "That's it. I won't get in any trouble for not coming forward right away, will I?"

"No, not at all. We're grateful you finally plucked up the courage to drop in and see us. We're going to need to take a statement from you, though, which we can arrange to take place in the future."

"At home, or will I have to come here?"

"It's entirely up to you; again, no pressure."

"You've been really kind to me. I was dreading coming here. I caught the press conference the other night and have had a few sleepless nights ever since. I kept dreaming about coming here to inform you and the two men coming after me, killing me for dobbing them in."

"I don't think that will happen, in fact, I'm pretty sure it won't. The odds of the men ever tracking you down are minimal, I can assure you. Shall I get an officer to come to your address for the statement?"

"Yes, can I leave it a day or two? Coming here today has been far more traumatic than I thought it would be. I'm not usually this much of a wimp. The thought of…" He lowered his head.

"Possibly discovering the dead body yourself, is that what you were going to say?"

"Yes, it makes me shudder. Do you know who the victim is yet?"

"Yes, we've made an identification, but that's about all at this stage."

"You have your work cut out for you. My uncle used to be a copper, back in the day. He often said that police work could be boring day in and day out, but once the pieces of the puzzle slotted together, that's when it became interesting."

"I can vouch for that. Which is why it's extremely important we hold the press conferences, in the hope that people like you, who have witnessed something out of the ordinary, come forward."

"I'm sorry, I regret not coming down here before this."

"No harm done in this case. We really appreciate you plucking up the courage to visit us today. I'm going to give you one of my cards in case anything else comes to mind when you leave us."

"Thank you. If it does, I'll call you right away."

"You do that. We'll leave you to finish your cup of tea, there's no rush. We need to get the ball rolling on the information you've given us today."

Lorne flicked to a clean page and slid the notebook across the table. "If you can jot down your name and address for me, we'll give it to the desk sergeant for him to organise obtaining a statement from you."

He wrote his details clearly in the notebook and passed it back to Lorne.

She read it and smiled. "Thanks."

Sally and Lorne rose from their seats. At the door, Sally turned back and thanked Kai for having the courage to come in and see them.

"My only regret is that I didn't do it sooner. I think it was the unknown. I had to conquer my fears of having to deal with the police first."

"We're not all grumpy old men, as you can tell."

He smiled. "Far from it. Thank you both for being gentle and understanding with me."

"You're welcome. Take care, and my advice would be to stick to the open roads at that time of night in the future."

"Thanks for the advice. Funny that, I'd already worked it out for myself."

They left the door open, and Sally walked across the reception area to speak with the desk sergeant. "Pat, he managed to give us some valuable information. We're going to need to take a statement from him. Can I leave that with you to sort out?"

"Of course. Today or in the future?"

"In the next couple of days. Thanks."

Lorne entered her security number, and the door clunked

open. She held it ajar for Sally, and they climbed the stairs together.

"What's our first step for the day?"

"I want to bring the team up to date on what we've just discovered and then I think we should all knuckle down and see what we can come up with, and yes, I'm including myself in that, too."

"Blimey, you must be keen for a conclusion, if you're going to get your hands dirty."

"Hey, you, that was uncalled for. I get my hands dirty every day of the week, in one form or another."

"I know you do, I was only teasing. If we all get involved, then there's no reason why we shouldn't make good headway in the investigation today. I wonder who the men were who Kai saw leaving the woods."

"That's our priority. If we find out who they are... bingo, we'll get the investigation solved in no time at all."

"As easy as that, eh?"

"Believe that and you're dafter than I think you are." Sally smirked, getting her own back on her partner for her earlier impertinence.

They entered the office, and Sally asked for everyone's attention. She went over what they'd learned from Kai, and the team listened intently without interrupting her.

"Interesting. I know what you're going to ask next, boss, about the CCTV or ANPR cameras in the area," Jordan said.

"And your reply would be?" Sally grinned at the young detective constable.

"It's out in the sticks, so it's very unlikely there will be any out that way."

Sally stared at him.

His cheeks reddened. "But I'll do my best."

"That's what I want to hear, Jordan."

"Joanna, can you do the necessary background checks on

Vanessa Kitten and her boyfriend, Carl Spencer? See if either of them has any kind of police record."

"Roger, boss."

"Stuart, I need you to research how many black or dark blue vans there are operating in the area. Initially, I want you to focus on the trades, in particular painters and decorators. If nothing shows up, then broaden your search. Don't forget the partial number plate."

"Gosh, that's right. Within what radius, boss?"

"Let's do a twenty-mile radius, using the woods as the epicentre."

Stuart nodded.

"Right, that leaves us to go through the social media side of things. Lorne, are you up for it?"

"Bring it on. Together or separately so we can compare notes later?"

"Separately. I'll carry out my checks in my office, once I've flicked through the post that has landed on my desk overnight. Who do you want to concentrate on?"

"I'll take Vanessa if you like. I think women tend to be more interested in posting than men."

"We'll see about that. Okay, we've all been given our tasks, work smart, peeps."

"A quick one before you go, boss," Joanna called out.

Sally turned to face her. "What's that?"

"Do you want me to check out the builder as well? Bearing in mind what the witness said."

Sally raised a finger. "Good thinking. The more we do at this stage the better." She continued her walk to her office and breathed out a weary sigh as she sat behind her desk.

I'm tired before the day begins, what's that all about? It's cases like this that really get the mind working, which can be draining. I hope some good news comes our way soon.

. . .

A FEW HOURS LATER, Sally called the team together to get an update. "With the exception of Jordan, I know the camera side of things will take the longest to research, has anyone managed to find anything out yet?"

Joanna half-raised her hand. "There's nothing on the police records for Vanessa, Spencer, or the builder, Robin Askew."

"Fair enough. There's a chance I'm guilty of barking up the wrong tree about them, although, saying that, I don't think Vanessa or her boyfriend should be dismissed outright just yet. Does anyone else agree?"

"Absolutely, if only because they were seeing each other when Vanessa was still living with Dan," Lorne replied.

Sally nodded. "Did you find anything of note in her social media? I have to say, I was extremely disappointed with what I read on his feed. It was all about fitness and well-being. Lots of adverts for events going on up and down the country to do with weightlifting. The lack of personal stuff was a bitter disappointment."

"Hmm... Vanessa was the total opposite. She posted anything and everything about her social life. I found the post she made to announce moving in with Dan. It was accompanied by a picture of them, kissing and appearing to be very happy together. I also spotted the announcement she made when Dan went missing. She put a call out, rallying her friends; some of them offered to give up their evenings and help search for him for up to a week after he disappeared. Her timeline was filled with sad memes for a while, but that all changed when she revealed she was seeing Carl Spencer. Most of her friends left comments saying how pleased they were for her, but there were also a few snarky comments from a few men, slating her for moving on so quickly. I checked out who the people were, and they turned out to be Dan's mates."

"Interesting. Still nothing much to go on, not really. I think if Vanessa had done away with Dan, the last thing she would do is highlight it on Facebook, would she?"

"Hard to say at this time," Lorne said.

"We'll come back to it, if nothing else comes our way. That leaves you, Stuart. Is it too soon for you to have any news for us about the van?"

"I'm getting there, boss. I could do with another couple of hours to complete my research. I'd hate to give you only half the information and omit something important in the process."

"You've got until the end of the day, Stuart, will that be long enough?"

"Plenty, I'd say. Thanks, boss."

"Jordan, about the cameras in that area, where are the closest ones?"

"I'd say about five miles on either side of the woods, that's what I have been focusing most of my efforts on for the past hour or so."

"Has anything come of that yet?"

"Nothing. But I'm not surprised, I know from experience how long it can take to gather any worthwhile evidence from the limited cameras in the area."

"Try not to get too frustrated with the task. Let me know if you find anything, no matter how insignificant you deem it. Anything you come up with is bound to be better than what we have at our disposal now."

"Will do."

Sally made the team a coffee each and distributed them. It gave her a chance to peer over their shoulders at the information they had written down at the same time. She was proud of what the team had accomplished so far, even though nothing of value had come from it.

"How's it going?" Sally pulled up a chair and sat next to Lorne.

Lorne angled her screen in Sally's direction. "I'm going through the friends' profiles at the moment. Some of them lead back to Dan's page."

"Was there anything worth reading on his page?"

"Not really. He wrote a post every so often. He mainly featured the properties he had renovated, letting his friends and family know his progress. Quite a few of them commented, told him he was doing a remarkable job and wished him luck with achieving the sale for each of the properties. I haven't picked up on any jealousy or malice towards him."

"It's all rather puzzling, isn't it? Why has it taken two years for his body to show up? Why not leave it where it was? Why freeze him in the first place?"

"All good questions that I suppose we'll discover the answers to eventually. All we need is a glimmer of hope to go on, and we're not at that stage yet."

"More's the pity. How long will it take for us to get there?"

"Here we go… you might as well be asking how long a piece of string is while you're at it. Or better still, ask me to look into my crystal ball."

"I know, I'm sorry. Hey, that's not a bad shout. I wonder if your psychic friend, Carol, would be able to lend us a hand."

"Now that's definitely worth considering, however, I think it's too early to give her a call just yet."

"If you say so. Do you think she'd be up for it? If we draw a blank by the end of the week?"

"I can sound her out, if that's what you want. It's been a few months since I've contacted her, she'll be thinking we've forgotten all about her."

"It's not your fault, time flies for all of us. We'll revisit the idea in a day or two, then. Okay, for now, let's keep digging. Something has to surface soon, doesn't it?"

"You'd hope so. What happens if it doesn't? Where do we turn next?"

"If calling on Carol is out of the question, I refuse to think about it. I'll keep my fingers crossed that something turns up for us soon, otherwise we're snookered. I don't think I've ever said that about a case before. I'd rather not think negatively about it either, that kind of mindset never gets a copper anywhere, does it?"

"So true."

SOMETIME LATER, Jordan, thankfully, came up trumps. "I've got something, here on this camera." He switched on the large TV screen, situated on the right of the room, and played the clip he'd sourced for everyone to see.

A dark van, Sally assumed was black, although it was difficult to see in the fading light, came into view and shot past the camera. "Can you perhaps get a close-up of the driver?"

"I can try." Jordan zoomed in, and the driver's blurred image filled the screen. "Damn, that's the worst thing about these cameras, the pixelation can be a pain in the rear."

Sally patted him on the shoulder. "Hey, you did your best. Okay, we'll set that aside for now. Can you concentrate on the number plate, Jordan?"

Jordan tinkered with the controls again, and this time the camera picked up the registration number of the vehicle, but again, the image was very grainy until Jordan successfully tweaked it a touch.

"Bingo, can you get that number down, Stuart?"

"I've got it, mate. I'll check it against the list I have on the go."

The room fell silent as the team's expectations heightened.

"Here it is, the vehicle is registered to Dick Pratt, he's a builder."

Sally wandered around the room, high-fiving the other members of the team. "Shit, time is getting on, it's almost four. I'm guessing the builder is on site somewhere and not likely to be at home at this time of the day. The last thing we want to do is show up at his address in force, only for him not to be there."

"What are you suggesting? That we work longer to catch him at home?" Lorne asked.

"Yes, is everyone okay with that?"

The team all nodded.

"Make the necessary calls to your loved ones, telling them you're going to be maybe a couple of hours late."

Sally rushed into her office to call her husband. "Hi, it's me. Don't bother cooking early tonight, we have to follow up on a lead but we're not going to be able to do it until maybe six or seven."

"Well, that sounds good. Okay, I'll make a casserole and put that in the oven for later. Does Tony know?"

"I presume Lorne is on the phone with him now. Are you at different locations?"

"Yes, he told me he was feeling a lot better, so we decided to split up to complete the snagging lists on the two properties that should be going on the market on Monday. Our builder assured us his men would work over the weekend to get the properties finished. It's going to cost, but the sooner we can get them on the market the better. Sorry, I'm holding you up chuntering on."

Sally laughed. "Nonsense, I love hearing about your day. Sounds like the dream team have pulled another blinder, yet again."

"It's not done and dusted just yet. But yes, the men have been putting in the extra hours to get both houses ready in time. I've promised them a couple of hundred each in bonuses, if they can pull it off."

"Great stuff. Okay, I'm going to love you and leave you now."

"Good luck. Keep me informed of your progress, if you get the chance."

"Of course." Sally ended the call and rejoined the team.

Everyone said they'd cleared the extra hours with their nearest and dearest.

"Okay, let's formulate a plan for this evening. Lorne, can you look up Pratt's Facebook page? Check if he mentions what job he's working on at present."

"On it now."

"Jordan and Stuart, you go ahead of us, stake out his home, just in case he decides to finish early. I suppose it's not unheard of for a builder to clock off late afternoon in some cases, depending on what job they're involved with during the day."

"Want us to set off now, boss?" Stuart asked.

"You might as well. Keep in touch."

"Joanna, I want you to stay here. Can you carry out the background checks on the individual? See if anything shows up or if there is a connection with the deceased."

"Rightio, boss."

Jordan and Stuart left the office.

Sally meandered over to Lorne's desk, to see what information she had gathered, if anything. "How's it going?"

"Give me a chance, I've only been at it five minutes."

"I know, I hate heaping the pressure on you like this, but..."

"Stop, I was joking. I've located his page, eventually. He

doesn't really have much to say for himself and rarely discusses what jobs he's working on at any given time."

"That's a shame. Can you see if Dan is on his friends list?"

"That was what I checked first of all, he isn't."

"Damn, I thought we might be on to something there."

"I'll check Companies House, see what I can unearth."

"Good shout."

Lorne followed Sally into her office five minutes later to share the results. "Seems like he has a decent business. He's made a profit year on year for the last five years. He's been trading for a decade."

"That's great, thanks, Lorne. Have Stuart and Jordan checked in yet?"

"Not yet. Want me to see where they are?"

"Might be a good idea." Sally glanced at her watch; it was already four-thirty. "They should have reached the location by now."

Lorne left the office and returned moments later. "They're a few streets away."

"Great. My stomach is full of butterflies, not something that happens often."

"You're not alone, mine's turning somersaults, as well. I hope it's because we're going to make a breakthrough this evening."

"Me, too. It's a matter of us sitting and waiting until the boys let us know when Pratt is at home."

"Hopefully we won't have to wait too long."

As it turned out, they didn't have long to wait at all. Jordan let them know that Pratt had arrived home at five-thirty. Sally and Lorne set off right away, only to get stuck in the evening rush-hour traffic.

Sally slammed the heel of her hand against the steering wheel. "Damn, why does this always happen when we're in a hurry?"

"It's called sod's law. You're going to need to use your blues and twos to get us there quickly."

Sally grinned and hit the siren. "You can take the blame if anyone puts in a complaint."

"They won't, and yes, that's fine by me. I don't give a shit, as long as we can get there quickly."

When the car in front of her crept forward, Sally eased out of the gap. She gave the driver the thumbs-up and weaved between the traffic on both sides of the main road until the roundabout appeared ahead. The traffic cleared once they were halfway around it, and their onward journey became easier, so Sally knocked off the siren and the lights.

"The satnav says we're ten minutes away," Lorne said. "It can't come quick enough for me. I'm dying to see what this man has to say for himself. I bet he thought he and his accomplice would get away with dumping the body in the woods, bloody numpties. I swear if some criminals had half a brain cell, they'd be a danger to themselves as well as the rest of society."

Sally chuckled. "I fear you're right. I hope he doesn't put up a fight. I forgot to sign out a Taser and I doubt if Jordan remembered to pick one up before he left the station, either. That's my fault, I should have reminded him."

"Nonsense, you're worrying about nothing. With four coppers showing up on his doorstep, Pratt's hardly going to do a runner, is he?"

Sally glanced at her partner and hitched up an eyebrow. "Stranger things have happened. Who knows these days how someone is going to react when they feel they've been cornered?"

The house was a semi-detached in need of repair to the wall at the front and the windowsills, downstairs and upstairs. The van was parked on the drive—that too was in need of repair.

Sally pulled up outside a house a couple of doors down from Pratt's. Jordan and Stuart left their car and jumped into the back of Sally's. There, the four of them discussed their plan of action.

"I think we should all show up at the front door. I know ordinarily we'd split up, two taking the front and the other two at the back, but I think this will be a better way to proceed, don't ask me why."

"I wholeheartedly agree," Lorne chipped in. "Stuart and Jordan can chase after Pratt if he tries to escape through the back door."

"Oh, cheers. Maybe we should have put our trainers on instead, mate," Jordan piped up.

Sally peered over her shoulder and grinned at the young constables. "Any objections?"

"None."

"Okay, let's make our move. Keep a watchful eye on the windows. If he spots us, that's when he could make a run for it."

The four of them left the car. Sally and Lorne took the lead and walked up the cracked concrete path to the house. There was no bell fitted, so she used the knocker positioned on the centre panel of the flaking green door.

A woman in her early forties, wearing a vibrant pink velour leisure suit, opened it moments later. "Yes, can I help?" Her gaze flitted nervously between them all.

Sally showed her ID and introduced herself. "We're here to see Mr Dick Pratt. Is he at home?"

"Who is it, Lisa?" A man appeared behind the woman in the hallway. He saw Sally and her colleagues standing on the doorstep and bolted.

"Wait right there, Pratt. I wouldn't advise you to go out that way, we've got officers around the back as well... I said stay where you are!" Sally shoved past his wife and then stood aside, allowing Stuart and Jordan to rush past her to give chase to the suspect.

"Hey, now wait just a minute, you can't come in here uninvited, I know my rights. You're trespassing."

"We can when there's a murder suspect in the house, Mrs Pratt," Sally had pleasure in correcting her.

"A what? You're mistaken, he hasn't murdered anyone. What the fuck makes you think that? You've got to be out of your minds, he hasn't got it in him for a start. Oi, are you listening to me? Get out of my house or I'm going to ring the station and put in a complaint."

Jordan caught up with the escapee, twisted his arm up his back and returned to the hallway with him. He read the suspect his rights, and Stuart helped Jordan to snap the cuffs in place.

"You can't do this, I've done nothing wrong. There must be some kind of mistake," Pratt objected.

Sally noticed how the man was avoiding any form of eye contact with his wife.

"Yes, there must be a mistake. He wouldn't do it, you have to believe me, even if you don't want to believe him," his wife insisted.

"We'll take him down the station and interview him, either this evening or possibly first thing in the morning," Sally told the distressed woman.

"I'm not in the habit of lying. If I tell you he's innocent, then that's the truth."

Sally shook her head and tutted. "I'm sorry, but the evidence we have discovered tells a very different story." She was careful not to give too much away and deliberately kept the fact that a witness had given them the lead to find him in the first place.

"Don't worry, Dick, I'll give my brother a call, he'll know what to do."

"You idiot, Jeff won't know because he's a property solicitor. I need a criminal lawyer to stand beside me."

"Do you want my help or not?" His wife challenged him. Pratt nodded. "Then I'll call him right away, he'll know who to contact."

"Whatever. You have to believe me, Lisa, I didn't do this," Pratt shouted, his voice shaking.

Jordan and Stuart led him past his wife and Sally and Lorne, who all stood back in the confined hallway.

"Listen to him, he's panicking. I'm telling you, you've got the wrong man," his wife pleaded with tears streaming down her cheeks.

Sally swallowed down the lump that had emerged. "I'm sorry, the evidence tells us otherwise."

Lisa slumped onto the stairs and stared at Sally and Lorne. "He has never put a foot wrong in the twenty years I've known him. Please, why aren't you listening to me?"

"We are. If he cooperates with us, then…"

"Then what?" Lisa bounced to her feet again. "Will you let him go?"

"I'm sorry, I can't answer that until we've interviewed him. Sorry for disturbing your evening."

"No, you're not. Be honest with me, that was your intention all along."

"We've tried to track your husband down during the course of the day. Unfortunately, we didn't know where he was working, otherwise we would have brought him in for questioning earlier."

"What an utter shambles this is. He's innocent, I can say it until I'm blue in the bloody face, but you're not going to accept it, are you?"

Sally shrugged. Not wishing to get into an argument with the woman, she said, "We have to go now."

"This isn't the last you've heard about this. I'm warning

you, I'll get the press involved if I have to. That man is as innocent as a newborn baby. I'll see what my brother has to say about this. And don't go giving him one of your bloody duty solicitors, he needs someone impartial alongside him during the interview."

"I can assure you that all of our duty solicitors are impartial. But if you prefer to have a solicitor of your own during the interview, then fair enough. Why don't you arrange for them to be at the station by nine-thirty in the morning?"

"I'll get on the phone as soon as you're gone. Does that mean you're going to let him go tonight?"

"No, I'm sorry. He'll be spending the night in a cell."

"What a disgrace you are. How dare you swan in here and disrupt our lives like this?"

"I'm sorry you feel like that. I'm sure you can understand things from our point of view, knowing that your husband's name has come up during a murder inquiry."

"Who told you? I want to know who mentioned him and in what circumstances."

"I can't tell you that at the moment. Good evening, Mrs Pratt."

Once she'd left the house and was on her way back to the car, Sally blew out a breath. She flinched at the sound of the front door slamming behind them.

"I can't blame her for being narked. She seemed adamant that we'd got the wrong man," Lorne said almost warily.

"I know, but the evidence is telling us otherwise. You know how this works, partner."

"I do. I'm speaking honestly here when I say that her genuine disbelief has put a major doubt in my mind."

"Mine, too, if you want to know the truth. But you know as well as I do, the need for us to work with the evidence we have to hand."

Lorne nodded, and they climbed into the car.

"We'll get him settled for the night then call it a day."

"We're forgetting one thing."

Sally frowned and turned to face her partner. "What's that?"

"We should be arresting two men. What if his wife gets in touch with the other man? Informs him about her husband's arrest and he takes off?"

"Hmm… but according to Pratt, and his wife for that matter, he's totally innocent, so how likely is that going to be?"

"You're right, I should keep my mouth shut."

"What? No way. I wasn't having a pop at you, I was merely stating facts. I don't want us to fall out about this, Lorne. What if the wife really doesn't know her husband at all? What if he's in cahoots with his partner, a black man who remains a mystery to us? Maybe we should put in the extra hours tonight, to get the truth out of him. What do you think?"

"On the one hand, I think we should, but on the other, it makes more sense to hit him in the morning, when we're both fresher. It'll give us both a chance to make some notes this evening, that is, if you want me to?"

"Of course I do. In fact, that would be a massive help. You know how much I value your input, especially when we appear to have our backs against the wall."

"It'll be interesting to hear what he has to say during the interview tomorrow."

"And what his reaction is to hearing the news that he's going to spend the night in the cells."

Sally smiled and drew away from the kerb. Stuart followed them back to the station where they booked Pratt in with the custody sergeant.

"Make yourself comfortable, Mr Pratt. We'll interview you in the morning."

"What? You can't do this to me."

"I think you'll find we can." Sally grinned and nodded for the constable to take him away. She went upstairs, thanked the team for their hard work during the day and dismissed them. "Have a good rest this evening, folks. Tomorrow is another day. Depending on what Pratt has to tell us in the morning, we're still missing a major part of the puzzle, his partner in crime."

CHAPTER 5

The desk sergeant welcomed them the following day and reported that the suspect had been restless all night, pacing his cell until the early hours of the morning.

"We'll leave him half an hour or so. His solicitor is supposed to be coming in at nine-thirty. We'll see if anyone shows up and go from there. I suppose that will be dependent upon whether they're available. If that's a negative, then we'll have to put in a request for the duty solicitor to attend."

"Let me know if and when you need me to contact anyone," Pat said.

"We will. See you in a little while." Sally tapped her code into the keypad, and the door sprang open, allowing her and Lorne to enter. "I'm going to leave the post until later. We'll make a coffee and compare notes in my office, if you're up for it?"

"Suits me, not that I have much to offer. By the time we'd finished dinner and cleared up after my late arrival home last night, it was already nine o'clock."

"Yeah, ditto. It was definitely an 'all work and no play'

kind of day. As I see it, our main priority seems to be interviewing Pratt and then rooting around in his past to see what we can come up with about his associate."

"Yeah, somehow, I don't think having a poke around his social media accounts is going to cut it, do you?"

"Sadly not."

They reached the main office and greeted the rest of the team.

"I hope everyone is in good spirits and had a restful evening yesterday because we're going to need to hit the ground running at full pelt this morning." Sally noted that the others all had a cup of coffee on their desks, so she didn't bother asking if they wanted one. She poured herself and Lorne a drink and then loitered at the door before they retired to the office. "We're going to spend the next thirty minutes going over the notes we made last night. I'd like everyone to carry on with the research they started yesterday into Pratt's background, with the intention of putting a name and face to his mysterious partner."

The team put their heads down, and Lorne followed Sally into her office. They sat opposite each other and opened up their notebooks.

"If Pratt doesn't speak to us after being banged up all night, I'm not sure where we go from here," Sally said.

"Hey, don't sound so down about it, Sal, it's still early days. Maybe we should call the lab, and see if they discovered any prints on the body, other than Pratt's, that we can run through the system."

"That's a great idea. I'll give them a call just before we go downstairs. Let me hear what you have."

"Nothing major, just the usual probing questions. It was still rankling me last night how shocked his wife was about his arrest."

"Me, too." Sally didn't get the chance to add anything else because her phone rang. "DI Sally Parker. How may I help?"

"It's Pat on reception, ma'am. Just to let you know that Mr Daly has arrived, he's Pratt's solicitor."

"Gosh, he's eager. Okay, offer him a drink if you will, Pat. We'll be down shortly." Sally ended the call. "We won't have time to compare what we've got now because his solicitor has arrived."

"He's very keen, almost unheard of for them to arrive fifteen minutes early. We're just going to need to wing it, aren't we?"

Sally laughed. "Nothing new there, then. Come on, finish your drink, we might as well get this over and done with."

They emptied their cups and made their way back down the stairs. Mr Daly was a man in his fifties. He seemed familiar to Sally, but she couldn't recall where she'd seen the man before. She offered her hand and made the introductions.

"I'm DI Sally Parker, SIO on the investigation, and this is my partner, DS Lorne Warner. Thank you for coming here today."

"My pleasure. Any chance I can have a brief chat with my client before the interview begins?"

"Of course. Let me have a quick word with the sergeant." Sally smiled and approached the desk. "He wants to talk with Pratt before we interview him. Is there an interview room available?"

"Yes, I've cleared Room One for you to use. Want me to fetch Pratt now?"

"Thanks, that'd be great." Sally led Mr Daly down the corridor. "How long shall we give you?"

"Ten minutes should be enough. Is that okay with you, Inspector?"

"It's fine. He should be with you in a moment or two."

Sally retraced her steps back to the reception area and pointed at the exit. "Let's get some fresh air, while we're able to."

Outside, Lorne stood in front of Sally and asked, "Are you all right?"

"Yeah, sort of. I suppose I'm feeling a bit anxious, not sure why, when there is so much riding on us getting to the truth."

"I can understand you feeling apprehensive, Sal. Hey, you're going to need to draw on the positives; we've got him and his van on the footage, and the witness statement will back us up."

"I know. I simply can't kick this underlying feeling that all is not what it appears to be."

"Which is why we should get in there and see what he has to say for himself. There's no point in you tying yourself in knots before we hear his side of the story."

Sally paced the pavement, said hello to some of the officers arriving for duty, then drew in a deep breath and marched back through the main door. "Let's do this. Thanks for the pep talk, partner."

"Anytime. We've all been there over the years. My advice would be to take your time in there and make sure you pause between questions. If that means the interview takes longer, then so be it."

"You're a wise woman, Lorne Warner. Have I told you lately how much I appreciate you being by my side?"

Lorne smiled. "Yes, quite often, and the feeling is mutual. Now get in there and get the answers we need to wrap this bamboozling case up."

Sally mock-saluted her, and they walked down the corridor side by side.

She knocked on the door and poked her head into the room. "All right if we start the interview now, as time is marching on?"

Mr Daly gave a brief nod and smiled. "Yes. We're eager to get this over and done with as much as you are, Inspector."

"Can I order you both a drink before we start?"

"Thanks, another coffee wouldn't go amiss. What about you, Mr Pratt?"

"Jeez, what is wrong with you people? Can't we just get on with it? This is my life on the line, not yours, and I'd like to get this over and done with."

"Of course. Sergeant, perhaps you can arrange for the coffees to be sent through to us."

Lorne nodded and left the room. She returned after a few seconds and she and Sally took their seats at the table. Sally began the recording with the usual spiel.

"Okay, why don't we begin with you telling us what you were doing out at Wayland Wood on Monday evening, Mr Pratt, or may I call you Dick?"

"Either, I don't give a shit. Er… would you believe me if I told you I don't remember?"

"We have a witness who has made a statement to the effect that he passed you and another man some time around ten. Perhaps you can tell us who the other man was and where we can find him?"

After the briefest of pauses, Pratt said, "No comment."

"I've discussed this at length with my client, for some reason he is refusing to identify the other person seen in the woods," Mr Daly said.

"May we ask why?"

"He doesn't feel it would be appropriate at this time."

Sally frowned and asked Pratt, "Even if you solely go down for the murder of Dan Jessop?"

"I've already told you, I didn't kill anyone, and you have no proof that I have."

"Apart from the witness having seen you leaving the

woods after you dumped the deceased's body, yes, you're right."

"What proof do you have that my client dumped the body in the woods in the first place, Inspector? Maybe he was out for a walk to clear his head."

Sally put her hands out of sight under the table and crossed her fingers because she was about to tell a little white lie. "We have DNA evidence found on the body that is pointing us in Mr Pratt's direction." She turned her attention to Pratt. "It's only a matter of time before we catch up with your accomplice, therefore, it'll be in your best interests to give us his name."

Pratt whispered something behind his hand to his solicitor.

Daly then said, "Mr Pratt has told me that he doesn't want to name the other person who was with him for personal reasons."

"Personal reasons? So, you're admitting you weren't alone the night the deceased's body was dumped?"

Pratt sighed. "No, I wasn't. But I'd rather keep... my friend out of this."

"Even if it means that you will go to court, on trial for Dan Jessop's murder?"

"How many more times do I have to tell you, I didn't kill him? I didn't even know the man."

"Then tell us who did. Did your friend kill him and then ring you to assist with cleaning up the crime scene? Is that how this went down, Dick?"

"No, you've got this all wrong. Jesus, why won't you just believe me? I'm telling the truth."

"Because you're keeping the name of your accomplice from us. Give us his name and perhaps then we might start to believe you."

"I can't. He didn't do it either."

"So, you're trying to tell us you're both innocent and yet you were both seen leaving the crime scene area merely hours before the body was discovered. Forensics have your van. I'm predicting it will take them a couple of hours to come back to us with the evidence we need to arrest you for the murder of Dan Jessop. Why don't you tell us the truth and save us all a lot of time and hassle?"

"I am telling you the damn truth, I swear I am. I'm not denying…" He stopped speaking and dipped his head.

"You're not denying that you killed him or that you disposed of the body?" Sally immediately asked.

His head rose slightly, and his gaze met hers. "What's the point in me saying anything? You've already made up your mind that I'm guilty, despite lack of evidence."

"Lack of evidence? It'll come, sooner than you think. I'm expecting the final report back from Forensics later today. What we're doing here, is offering you the opportunity to tell us what really went on if, as you keep saying, you're completely innocent."

He shook his head half a dozen times and sighed. "Jesus, when you do someone a favour… why does it always have to come back and bite you in the arse?"

"A favour? So, you're admitting your accomplice, or your friend, was the one who killed Jessop."

"No, I've already told you, he didn't kill him either. Bloody hell, we're going round and round in circles here because you're deliberately not listening to me."

"Nothing could be further from the truth. I'm listening intently but I fear you're the one who is determined to go around in circles. First you tell us neither you nor your friend killed Dan Jessop, but then you're not denying dumping his body in the woods. Can you understand why I'm so confused right now?"

He flung himself back in his chair and stared at her. "This is your fault, we had all this worked out and…"

"My fault? What makes you say that?"

"You're twisting things, trying to get me to say something that I might regret later. All I did was…"

"We're listening. What did you do, Mr Pratt?"

"A friend a favour and look where it's got me? I didn't want all of this dropping on my doorstep," he muttered, his head bowed in shame once more.

"A favour? You're going to have to give us more than that if you want us to help you. How? By disposing of the body?"

"Yes. He was in trouble. Going out of his mind because there was a terrible smell at his house… no, I've said too much."

Daly leaned in to whisper something in Pratt's ear, and Lorne gave Sally's knee a gentle nudge under the table.

"Is there anything else you can tell us?" Sally asked. "We can work with you, if you're telling us you're both innocent. Why don't you tell us what happened, and we'll figure out what we can do to help you and your friend?"

"I don't think that will work. He's scared and he's not the only one. I never dreamt all of this would end up with me being arrested for murder. I hope you've done your background checks on me, I'm sure you'll soon realise what a grave mistake you're making."

"Are we? If you believe we're wrong about you, why don't you put the record straight and tell us what happened? We can help you, but we won't be able to do that if you don't confide in us."

He shook his head, and Sally noticed the tears welling up.

"I can't, he's a friend. Neither of us has done anything wrong."

"The evidence is proving otherwise. If you believe what

you're telling us, then why aren't you being more open with us?"

"Because I know how bad it looks for us. I can't dob my friend in. All we were doing was… the right thing. He had a problem and rang me to assist him."

"Okay, why don't we back up a bit here? You mentioned that there was a smell in his house, what type of smell?"

"A stench neither of us has ever smelt the likes of before. He asked for my help to try and find its source."

"And you obliged by going to his home, yes?"

"Yes. I thought he was talking about the kind of smell you get when your drains are backed up. I knew it couldn't be that as soon as I arrived at the house."

"Go on. What kind of smell was it?"

"We didn't have a clue, not at the time. E… my friend said he hunted high and low before I got there and then we turned our attention to the cellar. It was padlocked. He didn't have the key or the tools to open the door and asked me to do it."

"Hang on, how long had your friend lived with the smell?"

"He'd been away. He came home to the stench. The electricity had gone off while he was away. We had a blackout a few days before that, the switch had tripped, and that was when the body must have…"

"Thawed out?" Sally asked.

"Yes. When we ventured into the cellar, we discovered a chest freezer down there. It was obvious where the smell was coming from. Never in my wildest dreams did I think I'd ever find a body in there. We were both shocked. My friend was distraught, frantic, he was. I told him we should call the police, but he had a genuine reason why he couldn't."

"And that was?"

"You'll have to ask him that. It's not my place to say."

"Fair enough. Thank you for eventually being honest with us. Can you give us your friend's name?"

"What will happen to me?"

"We'll gather all the evidence and go from there. If you're telling us the truth, you will still face charges for disposing of the body. Whether it was intentional or not. You should have called nine-nine-nine and let us deal with the corpse, you didn't."

"I'm sorry. I know we should have, but Elijah… damn…"

"You might as well tell us his surname now. Look, the more you divulge the less sentence you're likely to serve."

"You're giving me false hopes, I know what you coppers get up to… you're always keen to fit innocent people up just so you can wrap a case up quickly."

"You're wrong. The police are there to prevent crimes like this ever happening. If, as you're insisting, this is a genuine mistake then it will be easily sorted, once all the evidence has been gathered. Is there any way Elijah could have killed Jesus?"

"He's not the type, and neither am I, I swear we're not. I know we're wrong to have got rid of the body, I didn't want to go down that route, but Elijah was scared stiff. The only reason I did it was to help out a friend, you have to believe me."

Sally smiled at him. "I do. Now, all we need is Elijah's full name and his address. We can wrap this case up today, if you give us his details."

"I don't know… he could be gone by now. I wouldn't blame him either. He was terrified of the police showing up."

"I don't understand why."

Lorne leaned in and whispered, "Could he be in this country illegally?"

Sally pulled back and nodded. "Is Elijah an illegal immigrant?"

"No, at least that's what he told me. Please, all of this is a huge mistake that fell into our laps. We didn't put the body in the freezer or lock that cellar, for God's sake. You're going to have to take my word for it. All this was a major shock for both of us. We freaked out, or should I say Elijah did, he's petrified of the police, and no, I don't know what's gone on in the past for him to think that way."

"It'll be interesting to find out. Where does he live?"

Pratt covered his face and groaned. "He's going to kill me... and all because I thought I was doing the right thing for him. What an absolute mess!"

"His address, Mr Pratt?"

"I hope he can forgive me. It's sixteen Manor Road, over in Hethel. Can't I go with you, to help soften the blow?"

"No, I don't think that would be advisable. Does Elijah work?"

"Yes, he's a teacher at St Joseph's. He's worked exceptionally hard to fit in at the school. Please, can't you wait until this evening? He'll be mortified if you spoil this opportunity for him."

"We'll be discreet, don't worry. Did you tell me his surname?"

"I don't think so, it's Abagun. You will be gentle with him, won't you? The last time I saw him he was bricking it."

"Have you seen or spoken to him since you dumped the body?"

"No, I've been up to my neck in work all week, my wife will vouch for me."

"We believe you. Although, I'm very surprised you haven't been in touch with him since."

"Busy workload, no other reason. I still regard him as my mate, nothing has changed in that respect. There was no malice intended when we dumped the body. Overnight, whilst sitting in my cell, I realised we were foolish to go ahead with the idea. It was a spur-of-the-moment plan."

"Okay, it was still the wrong decision for you to make. I can't promise you won't end up serving time in prison."

Tears bulged, and the colour drained from his cheeks. "I can't believe it, even though we are both innocent?"

"But you're not, not really. You should have done the right thing and called the police. Situations like this aren't unheard of, and usually, if people feel they're innocent, they do the right thing and get in touch with us."

"It happened at the end of a long day for me; we were so panic-stricken, we weren't thinking straight. That's the only excuse I can give you. It was a genuine mistake and one that I will have nightmares about for the rest of my life."

"Inspector Parker, I believe my client has been fair and honest with you. He's told you the truth, and as far as I'm concerned, I believe he should be released. I don't think he can be considered a risk to society or a flight risk, do you?"

"I'm inclined to agree with you, but we won't be letting Mr Pratt go just yet, not until we've picked up Mr Abagun and questioned him. If he corroborates Mr Pratt's story, then yes, I'll let him go straight away."

Mr Daly opened his mouth to speak, but Sally raised her hand to stop him.

"I'm sorry, there's no point in you trying to talk me around, either. Your client still disposed of a dead body, even you have to admit that was the wrong thing to do."

Daly sighed and nodded. "Okay, but as soon as you pick Abagun up, will you promise to let my client go?"

"I will, although he'll be charged before he's set free. As long as Mr Pratt is clear about that then I have no issue about setting him free."

Tears spilled onto Pratt's cheeks, and he whispered, "But I didn't do anything wrong, not really. The man was dead already and stuffed in a freezer, and here I am, getting the blame for it. It doesn't make sense."

"I've given my reasons. I appreciate you've eventually told us the truth, but it wouldn't be right for me just to let you go with a slap on the wrist now, would it? Abandonment of a dead body is a crime in the eyes of the law."

Daly whispered something in Pratt's ear, and he shrugged.

"Okay, I know I was in the wrong, but please, I'm begging you not to punish me for just helping out a friend who was in dire need."

"All I can do is thank you for having the decency to admit what you did. I'll be having a word with my senior officer, see if we can come to some agreement with the Crown Prosecution Service about a lesser charge for you, how's that?"

Daly nodded. "Sounds fine to me. Thank you for being so considerate, Inspector."

"Yes, thank you," Pratt mumbled, his head bowed.

"Interview ended at eleven-ten a.m." Sally announced and switched the recording machine off, then smiled at the constable in the room. "Can you return Mr Pratt to his cell?"

The young officer stepped forward and tapped Pratt on the shoulder. "Come with me, sir."

Pratt said nothing further but held Sally's gaze as he stood.

Once he'd left the room, Daly pleaded, "I hope you were being honest and not giving Mr Pratt false hope, Inspector? I don't believe my client needs to spend time in prison over this matter, do you?"

"The decision is out of my hands, Mr Daly. As I've already stated, I will be doing everything I can to help Mr Pratt, but if everyone went around dumping dead bodies which they'd stumbled across, where would we be?"

"I appreciate how difficult this situation is, but there wasn't any malice or intent involved."

"Yes, I heard the argument Mr Pratt put forward. I'm sorry, we need to make a move now. Our priority is to pick up Mr Abagun ASAP. Hopefully, we'll have him sitting in a cell within the hour. Once he's been arrested then, and only then, will we let Mr Pratt go."

"Thank you, I'm sure he and his wife will both be grateful when he's finally released."

Sally and Lorne showed him back to the reception area and shook his hand.

"Thanks for coming in this morning."

"My pleasure. Thank you for treating my client fairly, in the circumstances."

Sally smiled, and then she and Lorne ran up the stairs to share the news about Abagun with the team.

"Joanna, can you do the necessary digging for me about him? Apparently, the men were too scared to call the police. Although Abagun is an immigrant, Pratt told me that he didn't think he was here illegally, but that statement isn't sitting well with me. According to Pratt, Abagun was panic-stricken when he suggested reporting the incident to the police."

"Leave it with me, I'll see what I can find out, boss."

"Right, I think we should all go to the school, just in case Abagun tries to run off. I'm in two minds about whether to take further backup with us."

"I don't believe that will be necessary," Lorne said. "Not if the four of us show up at the school. He wouldn't want to make a fool of himself in front of the kids, would he?"

"I hope you're right. Okay, let's make a move. I'm eager to see what Mr Abagun has to say for himself, if anything. There's a possibility he might go down the 'no comment' route. He'd be foolish if he did that, knowing that we already have Pratt sitting in a cell."

CHAPTER 6

The school was in Hethersett, approximately ten minutes from the station. Sally parked her car in a space close to the entrance, and Jordan drew into the row behind them. They met up outside the main door and entered the building.

Sally produced her ID and asked the receptionist if it was possible to speak with the head.

"I'm afraid Mrs White is in a meeting with a member of staff at the moment. Can you wait? She shouldn't be long."

Sally glanced at her watch. "We're in a rush. Any chance you can hurry things along for us?"

"I can try. She's bound to ask what your visit is regarding. What shall I tell her?" the older woman asked with an anxious smile.

"It's regarding a member of her staff. We're desperate to have a chat with him about a serious crime."

"Oh my, that doesn't sound too good. Let me see what I can do for you."

"Thanks."

The woman removed a crutch that was leaning against the wall beside her and hobbled up the hallway twenty feet or so.

"Crap, now I feel bad about making her move," Sally mumbled to Lorne.

"Don't be silly. She didn't seem to mind."

The receptionist returned, her smile still in place. "Mrs White will see you soon. She and Mrs Cox have one more issue to attend to before they draw their meeting to a close."

"Thanks very much for checking for us."

"You're welcome. It does me good to have a wander now and again, otherwise my hip is prone to seizing up."

Sally winced. "You look like you're in pain. Nothing too serious, I hope."

"I had a hip operation three months ago; it didn't go as expected. I'm waiting to be recalled to go under the knife again. Not ideal, but there are people out there far worse off than I am."

"Ouch, I hope they can put it right soon."

She returned to her desk and rested the crutch on the wall behind her.

Two women appeared in the hallway ahead of them.

"Here she is now. I'll introduce you, once she's free," the receptionist said in a hushed voice.

Mrs White smiled at the older woman she was speaking to and Mrs Cox walked off. "Now then, Anna, you mentioned there were some police officers here to speak with me?"

Sally held out her hand. "DI Sally Parker. These are my colleagues, DS Warner, DC Reid and DC McBain."

"Four officers, may I ask what all this is about? Wait, Anna said that your visit was to do with a member of my staff and a serious crime. Can you tell me more?"

"Here or in your office?"

"In my office, but I'd prefer it if you and I spoke alone, Inspector, would that be all right with you?"

"Absolutely." Sally glanced over her shoulder at the rest of her team. "I shouldn't be too long."

Mrs White spun on her heel and strode back to her office with Sally having to walk briskly to keep up with the woman who was at least five inches taller than her, and that showed in her stride.

"Come in. I have a Zoom meeting in ten minutes, just so that you're aware."

"I won't take up too much of your time. We're here to have a chat with Elijah Abagun. Is he on the premises today?"

"What? May I ask what he is supposed to have done?"

"He's carried out a serious crime, that's all I'm prepared to say for now. Is he here today?"

"Yes, as far as I know. Goodness me, what on earth has he done wrong? He's the meekest man I know. A true gentleman in every respect. He's wonderful with the children, too. Seriously, you've confounded me with your accusation. Are you sure you've got the right man?"

"Categorically. His accomplice is at the station now. He's told us what happened, hence our reason for being here today," Sally said, guarded with how much she revealed to the headmistress.

Mrs White shook her head in disbelief. "I'm struggling to make any sense of this. Elijah is so polite, such a gentle man but, if you have evidence to the contrary, who am I to stand in your way?"

"Thank you. Is he teaching a class at the moment?"

"Yes, I'm understaffed today, two teachers have called in sick. Is there any way you can delay speaking to him until twelve, when the lunch bell rings?"

Sally glanced at her watch. It was eleven-fifty. "That's fine, we don't mind hanging around for ten minutes. Is there somewhere we can wait, or would you rather we hang around in the reception area?"

"I can take you to the staffroom, we don't have any other rooms free at present."

"We'd rather speak with him in private, although, just to warn you, we will be taking him in for questioning."

"My oh my, but I've already told you that I have several members of staff off today. Can't you question him after the school day has ended?"

"Sorry, no. I understand how inconvenient this is for you, but we're talking about Mr Abagun being involved in a *very* serious crime."

Mrs White placed her hands on either side of her face and shook her head. "What about in my office? No, no, that won't work, I have a few online meetings I need to attend over the next thirty minutes. Sorry, I'm not trying to cause problems for you."

"It's okay. Please don't worry. Can you tell me where his classroom is?"

"It's on the other side of the school, it might take you a few minutes to get there. Elijah usually goes directly to the staffroom once he's finished his lesson. Maybe it would be better for you to wait for him there."

"And where is the staffroom?"

"It's at the end of the hallway. I can take you there, I have enough time before my meeting."

"That would be great. We'll try not to cause too much of a fuss. Of course, it all depends on what Elijah's reaction is going to be when I announce who we are and why we're here to speak with him."

"I've never been in this situation before. I hope it doesn't cause too much disruption. Well, it's going to because I'll have to arrange for someone to cover Elijah's next class. Let me worry about that later, let's get you and your colleagues to the staffroom for now."

They left the office. Outside, Sally gestured for the others to follow them down the hallway. They met up outside the staffroom. Mrs White told them to make themselves comfortable and swiftly left the room.

Sally brought the rest of the team up to date on what was going on.

"It's going to be a bit awkward, if the rest of the staff are in here when he arrives," Lorne said.

"You're right, maybe this isn't ideal, waiting for him in this room. What if we wait in the hallway instead?"

"I think that's going to be just as bad," Lorne replied.

"I'm open to suggestions."

"I haven't got an alternative, sorry. What about you two?" Lorne asked Jordan and Stuart.

They both shrugged and shook their heads.

"This will have to do then." Sally checked her watch again. "Two minutes before the bell rings. Maybe Lorne and I should take a seat, and Jordan, you and Stuart, you could stand off to the side. If he clocks us all together, he's bound to freak out."

"Sounds like a good idea," Jordan agreed.

He and Stuart took up their positions over by the bookcase which was closer to the door than the seating area on the right.

They sat there, twiddling their thumbs until the first member of staff entered the room. The young woman stopped in the doorway, and her gaze flitted between them.

"Should you be in here?" she asked nervously.

Sally flashed her warrant card. "We have Mrs White's permission. Don't let us stop you from enjoying your lunch."

"Okay, but why are you here? Or aren't you allowed to tell me?"

"We're waiting to have a chat with a member of staff. Mrs White is on a conference call, otherwise she'd be here with us. There's no reason for you to be alarmed."

"Isn't there? With four police officers lurking in our staffroom?"

Sally smiled, and the door opened behind the young teacher. Two more females entered the room. The first teacher to arrive let the others know what was going on.

They all filtered further into the room. One lady made herself and her colleagues a drink, while the others collected food from the fridge, then they all took a seat at a table, a few feet away from Sally and Lorne.

A white male entered next. He wasn't alarmed to see the officers, just went about his business as if nothing was wrong.

The door opened again, and this time a black man took one look in Jordan and Stuart's direction and bolted.

"Was that Elijah Abagun?" Sally asked the women eating their lunch a few feet away.

"Yes," one of them said through a mouthful of sandwich.

The four of them dashed out of the room, in hot pursuit of the suspect.

"Which way did he go, left or right?" Sally asked.

"No idea, he was too fast for us," Jordan said.

"We're going to need to call for backup," Lorne advised.

"Can you do that, Lorne?"

Lorne withdrew her phone and placed the call.

"Why don't you go right? We'll go left once Lorne has finished on the phone."

Jordan and Stuart tore down the hallway as if their feet were on fire.

Lorne completed her call and said, "They're on their way. What if we don't catch him?"

"It's too early for negative thoughts to cross our minds. If he runs from here the likelihood is that he'll go home. Either way, he won't get away from us. Come on."

"I hope you're right."

They ran to the end of the corridor. The door in front of them was open.

"I think we've made the right call. Can you ring Stuart? Tell him to join us outside."

"What? While I'm running?"

"Crap, okay, I'll do it." Sally fished her phone out of her pocket and rang Stuart as she sprinted closer to the doorway. She poked her tongue out at Lorne. "Glad one of us still has the dexterity to carry out two tasks at the same time."

"Piss off," Lorne growled between breaths.

Sally grinned. "Stuart, we've located an open door at the end of the hallway. Can you meet us outside?"

"Bugger. I mean yes, we're out the front, checking out the car park."

"Stick with that for now. I'll give you a call back if we find him."

"Likewise, boss."

Sally ended the call, and she and Lorne upped their pace slightly until they made it outside the building.

"Do you know this area?" Lorne asked.

"Not enough. I'm trying to get my bearings."

"The field ahead of us looks like it might belong to the school. There are several goalposts in the middle."

"You're probably right. Would he head out into the open like that, if he came this way?"

"Then why don't we search the immediate area around the school building first? We can broaden the search when backup arrives."

"Makes sense. Come on, instinct is telling me to go left here."

They raced down the side of the building which led them back to the car park and the main entrance where they met up with Stuart and Jordan who were still busy checking behind all the stationary vehicles.

"Jordan, Stuart, have you seen him?"

"That's a negative. We're checking the final row of cars now," Stuart replied.

"Okay, we've got backup on the way. Lorne and I will keep searching the grounds closest to the building."

The two men gave her the thumbs-up, and they continued their search.

"Let's pop our heads into the reception area, and see if they've seen him."

The receptionist seemed terror-stricken. "Have you found him? A member of staff told me he'd run off."

"No, the door was open at the end of the corridor." Sally glanced that way. There was a bend up ahead, blocking the receptionist's view. "You wouldn't see it from here. Is the door alarmed?"

"It should be. The maintenance guy told me to put in a call yesterday, but the contractors aren't due for another couple of days."

"Not to worry. Are there any other buildings on site that the staff have access to?"

She sat and mulled the question over. "No, I can't think of anywhere... no, that's not true, there's a cabin over to the right, close to the school. The teachers use that sometimes for nature studies. I don't think it has been used recently, though."

"Do you have the key for it?"

Anna leaned forward and whispered, "If you look under the steps, there's a hook, the key is on that."

Sally rolled her eyes and tutted. "I expect better from a school of this calibre."

"Sorry, yes, I agree. It was Martin, our handyman's idea, we've never had any issues with it. All the teachers know the key is there, but they discreetly collect it before the pupils arrive for their class."

"Left or right at the front door?"

"Right."

"Sorry, you did say. If you see Elijah, can you raise some kind of alarm for us? No, forget that, we don't want to disrupt the school. Here's my card, can you give me a call on my mobile?"

"Of course. Good luck."

Sally and Lorne stepped outside again and almost bumped into Jordan and Stuart. "We've got a possible hiding place for him. We should take a look together."

They rounded the building and saw the cabin. The door was closed. They spread out, not knowing if they could be seen approaching the cabin or not; they'd need to take a chance. Sally checked under the steps for the key—it was still there.

She slammed her fist against her thigh and cursed. "The key is still there. Where else could he be?"

"Do we know if he's got a car?" Jordan asked.

"If he had, we weren't that far behind him and we would have seen him drive off," Stuart suggested.

"But what if he's hiding behind a bush or a tree, observing us? Once we get out of sight, he could double back to his car and drive off," Lorne said.

"Good point. Jordan, can you go back? Keep an eye on the car park. Actually, on your way, pop your head into the reception area, ask Anna what car Abagun drives. If she knows, check the car park and get back to me."

Jordan tore away from them.

"I'm open to suggestions, guys, feel free to chip in with any ideas."

Before either Lorne or Stuart could answer, two patrol cars raced past them and stopped by the main entrance. Sally waved to get their attention, but the four officers entered the building. Seconds later, the men came to join them.

"Thanks for coming out, guys. We've got a black male on the run, height around six feet, slim build. He's a teacher at the school, so he's likely to know the area pretty well. He's a person of interest in a murder inquiry; we don't know if he's armed or not. We've checked the car park and this side of the building. We should spread out. There's a playing field at the rear, I think he'll head over that way as a last resort. What we need to do is search behind all the shrubs and hedges in this area. My team were right on his tail, so I can't imagine that he'll have got very far."

The team spread out and began their search. Ten minutes later, they came together again close to the main entrance.

"He must have gone across the field at the back, despite us initially ruling it out," Lorne suggested.

Sally scanned the area again and sighed. "I guess we need to relocate the search to out the back."

The group started moving up the side of the building to the playing fields at the back. There, Sally divided the team up into couples and gave them a section each to check out. Sally and Lorne took the closest area of bushes on the left. They searched deep inside the thorny stems of the roses, the berberis and the pyracantha bushes until something in the middle caught Sally's eye. Lorne blew a whistle she carried in her pocket for emergencies, alerting the others. The rest of the team joined them.

"Come out, Elijah, we've got you surrounded," Sally shouted.

The bushes rustled, and the suspect cried out in pain as he tried to stand. "Ouch, I can't move. Ouch, please help me!"

Lorne pointed at what appeared to be a sturdy branch lying on the grass beneath a nearby tree. "We could use that."

Sally nodded, and Lorne crossed the freshly trimmed lawn to fetch it.

"We might do some damage to the bushes, the head isn't going to like that," Lorne said.

"Tough. She can take it out of Abagun's salary."

"Yes, I'll pay, just get me out of here. I'm trapped, every time I move, the thorns attack me."

"All right, hold still, we'll get you out soon."

"Has anyone got any thick gloves with them?" Sally's question was directed at the uniformed officers.

"I've got some in the car, I could run back and get them," the youngest officer said.

"If you would. Make it quick."

The officer ran back to his vehicle and returned slightly out of breath. Then, he offered, "Do you want me to do it, ma'am?"

"Go for it but be careful."

The officer smiled and said, "I intend to be."

He ended up making light work of the task and created a path through the bushes which enabled Elijah to stand and exit the shrubbery safely.

"Thank you," he said over and over.

"Elijah Abagun, we're arresting you for disposing of a body which you discovered at your property. You do not have to say anything, but it may harm your defence if you do not mention when questioned something which you later rely on in court."

"I didn't do it... please, I didn't kill him," was Elijah's repeated mantra as they led him to the car.

"We'll talk more at the station. Don't say anything else,

not without a solicitor being present," Sally warned him. She nudged Lorne and whispered, "Can you ring the station, and get the duty solicitor organised?"

"Of course." Lorne dropped back to make the call.

Elijah was put in the back of one of the patrol cars. The rest of them followed in a convoy. Once they were settled in Sally's vehicle, Lorne high-fived her.

"Great job."

Sally grimaced. "You reckon? Now all we need to do is get the truth out of him. What if he didn't kill Jessop?"

"Then we're up shit creek, but it won't be the first time in our careers, will it?"

"Ain't that the truth? I have to admit, the poor bloke looks shit-scared of us. Makes you wonder what he had to put up with in his own country."

"It does. I guess we're going to find out soon enough."

When they reached the station, Pat informed them that the duty solicitor was going to be delayed for a while, which wasn't ideal. "It is what it is. Pat, can you get a doctor to check him over? I think he's got some nasty cuts all over him, judging by the amount of blood on his clothes."

"I can do that for you now."

"Thanks. Jordan and Stuart are checking him in. Let me know when the solicitor arrives, if you would?"

"You'll be the first one I call... er, the only one I call, even."

They all laughed.

Sally and Lorne left the reception area and made their way upstairs to the main office. They filled Joanna in about how the arrest had gone down.

"If backup hadn't arrived, we probably wouldn't have found him."

"Glad that wasn't the case. Has he had anything to say for himself?"

"Very little. Apparently, he kept quiet in the back of the car; there was the odd sniffle here and there. Once the doctor has seen him and given us the go-ahead to interview him, I have a feeling the truth is going to pour out. Let's face it, he'd be foolish if it didn't. How did you get on with his background checks?"

"According to his Facebook page, he moved to this country five years ago from Nigeria. I've found no evidence to say he's illegal, all his paperwork appears to be genuine. He was a maths teacher back in Nigeria. He's worked as a supply teacher since coming to the UK, but I think St Joseph's school have offered him something more permanent, if I read his post properly. I'll show you what I mean." Joanna brought up Elijah's Facebook page and pointed out the post.

"Hmm… I see, yes, not the best use of English in the world. Okay, it's something we can try and get out of him during the interview. Could you find any connection with Dan Jessop?"

"Nothing at all. He's got about thirty friends on his page. I've checked through as many as I could and still haven't come up with a possible link to the victim."

Sally sighed and nodded. "Okay, thanks, Joanna. Once the boys get back, I think we need to plan what our strategy should be going forward."

"Would it be worth checking out who the previous tenants were at the address?" Lorne asked.

Joanna smiled. "Great minds! I should have said, I've already started making a list from the electoral roll."

Lorne winked at Joanna. "You're always super-efficient, Joanna. Well done you."

"You took the words out of my mouth, Lorne. Keep up

the good work, Joanna. What about the owner of the property? I don't suppose you've had a chance to find out who that is, have you?"

"Not yet, I'm still searching for that one, no idea why it's taking me so long. That's why I thought I'd concentrate on the previous tenants instead. Maybe the suspect will give you a name during the interview. If he does, I can go hell for leather and carry out the necessary searches for them."

"As soon as he tells us, Lorne will text you the details, how's that?"

"Perfect, thanks, boss."

"I'm dying for a coffee. Lorne, will you do the honours while I make a start on the paperwork I set to one side this morning?"

"Umm… are you forgetting the time?" Lorne chewed her lip.

Sally frowned and cast her mind back to see if she'd forgotten anything that had been on her calendar for the day. "Sorry, you've lost me."

"It's lunchtime. We should take this opportunity to have something to eat before the duty solicitor arrives."

"Crap, yes, you're right. Can I leave that for you to deal with, while I make a start in my office? I'll have a ham and tomato on brown, either a roll or sandwich, I'm not bothered. I'll get some money for you."

"Don't be so insulting, this is on me. You've put your hand in your purse too much lately, for all of us."

Sally smiled. "Thanks, you're a gem."

Jordan and Stuart arrived. She left Lorne taking the rest of the orders for lunch and wandered through to her office. She sat in her chair and rested her head back.

The last few days have been full-on. Hopefully we'll be able to see the light at the end of the tunnel soon.

Rather than tackle her paperwork straight away, she gave Simon a call. "Hi, how's it going?"

"This is unusual to hear from you, is everything all right?"

"Is it? I think you'll find I reach out to you regularly during the week."

"My mistake. Yes, all is going well with us. We're putting the finishing touches to one property today; the estate agent is due later. The second property should be completed within the next few days; we've had a slight delay on that one. We've been trying to match the kitchen cabinets to those already installed in the property, but no one stocks them in the area and we can't be bothered searching the internet, not when it could hold us up, so we've decided to go with a black-and-white theme in there instead. Tony came up with the suggestion after we'd spent two days on the phone with the different suppliers in the area. Anyway, enough about me, how are you getting on with the investigation?"

"It's going. We have the main suspect sitting in a cell, we're just waiting on the duty solicitor to arrive."

"That's excellent news, and yet I'm not detecting any glee in your voice."

"You know me too well. There's something more to this case than meets the eye. I'll tell you all about it later. I just needed to hear your voice. Enjoy the rest of your day."

"Hey, before you hang up on me, are you sure you're okay, Sal?"

"I'm fine. Love you, see you later."

"I'll pick up something special for dinner tonight, we'll have a proper chat then, and I love you, too. Don't ever forget that, either."

"I won't, you're a very special man, Simon."

"Ditto. I mean… well, you know what I mean. My life has totally changed for the better since I met you."

"You old charmer." She blew a kiss down the line and hung up. In truth, both their lives had changed for the better since they'd started seeing each other.

Ten minutes later, Lorne interrupted her mindless chore of going through the daily post when she fetched Sally her roll and a coffee.

"Thanks, partner. Why don't you eat your lunch in here with me?"

"I'll go and get it. Are you all right? You seem a bit down."

"No, lost in thought maybe, but definitely not down. What would I have to feel down about?"

"I don't know. I'll get my lunch and we can discuss it."

Sally nodded and opened the bag to remove her ham and tomato roll.

Lorne entered the room, left the door open and sat in the seat opposite her. "Is the roll okay? You haven't touched it yet."

"Give me a chance, I wanted to fire off this last email before I started on my food. How are things going out there?"

"I checked in with Joanna, she's got a few names on the list of previous tenants already."

"That's great news. It's always good to have a backup plan in place. That doesn't mean that Elijah is off the hook, far from it."

"I totally agree with you. Why are men such dickheads?"

"Christ, not that old chestnut. I think women from as far back as the Ice Age have probably asked the same question over the years and are still seeking a satisfactory answer."

They both laughed.

"Seriously, though," Lorne continued, "it must be a man thing. You wouldn't find two women bricking it if they found a body in their cellar, would you?"

"I can't really answer that truthfully. I suppose we're

assuming most women would do the right thing and call the police to sort it out. In order for us to comprehend why Elijah panicked and rang Pratt, we need to have a better understanding of what he's been through in his life."

"Granted. I'm dying to find out what's going on in that head of his. Do you think we should have an interpreter with us during the interview?"

"I thought he appeared to speak good English. Do you think he'd be teaching in a school if his English was bad?"

"Fair point. It might be a good idea if we gave him the option. It's your call, though."

"After we've eaten, you can go down and ask him, see if he'd be happier with an interpreter or not."

"Jeez, thanks."

"My pleasure. You're the one who brought up the subject."

They tucked into their lunch, but Sally struggled to eat half of it because of the tightness gripping her stomach. "I can't eat any more. I just want to get on with the interview."

"Chill, it's going to be a little while yet. You should eat, it'll help you concentrate better when the time comes."

"Hark at you. Okay, just another few nibbles." Sally then revealed what Simon had said about the property they were renovating to put on the market.

"I knew my interior design skills would rub off on Tony sooner or later. I've never seen him so happy in his work."

"Simon is the same. Maybe we should consider joining forces with them in the future."

Lorne gave her a sideways glance. "Are you sure about that? Husbands and wives working together sounds like a murder investigation waiting to happen."

Sally sniggered. "You're nuts. Hey, we'd probably get away with it, too."

Frowning, Lorne asked, "How do you work that one out?"

"Because we're the best coppers around. The others aren't

a patch on us, so we'd more than likely succeed in burying our husbands under a patio together, or separately at different houses, whichever takes our fancy."

"Ah, gotcha. God, I don't ever want to consider killing Tony off." Lorne shuddered.

"I'm kidding. Where has your sense of humour gone lately?"

"It's there, just buried deeper these days."

"I can understand that, I suppose, after what we went through with Simon and Tony a few months ago. We could have lost them both, and here we are, talking about killing them off and burying them under the patio."

"Sally, stop taking things so seriously, this isn't like you at all. Come on, tell me what's going on in that head of yours."

"Honestly, I wish I knew. I can't help wondering what lies ahead of us with this investigation. It's taken us long enough to work out and find the suspects who dumped the body. If they didn't kill Jessop, then who did? And how the heck are we going to find them?"

"Good old-fashioned detective work, like always. Don't be such a defeatist, this isn't like you in the slightest."

"I know. I suppose I'm getting tired of chasing the evidence all day long."

"What are you saying?" Lorne probed.

"Nothing, not really. I thought starting up the Cold Case Team would be a doddle, and to be fair, it was when it was initially formed to put right Falkirk's shit, but now all those cases have been dealt with, we've got mysteries like this to solve."

"Are you telling me you'd prefer an easier life these days? Rather than dealing with a challenging case that will tax your brain?"

Sally threw the rest of her roll in the bin. "Pass, ask me another. You know me, I'm never usually the one looking for the easy way out, maybe it's this case that is causing me to doubt what's going on up here." She tapped her forehead.

"You're being too hard on yourself. I know this hasn't been the simplest of investigations this far, but we're getting closer to finding out what the truth is, hang in there."

"Don't get me wrong, I'm not considering throwing in the towel, not yet. I suppose what I'm trying to say is that every murder inquiry is different, none of them can ever be classed the same, can they?"

"It's called life, and shit happens at times, which can steer an investigation in a different direction than we think it's logically going to take. I think that's what you're probably sensing with this case. In my opinion, it's too early to say whether that's true or not. Why don't you take a step back until we've had a chance to interview Abagun and then we can revisit this conversation afterwards?"

"You're talking a lot of sense and not for the first time."

"I do my best. Are you okay now?"

"I'm fine. Go on, shoo. Let me get back to finishing off this crap. By then, with any luck, the duty solicitor will have arrived."

Lorne rose from her seat and took the rest of her lunch with her. "I can take a hint. I was joking again before you bite my head off. I'll go and check on Elijah, and see if he needs an interpreter."

"Let me know how he's doing when you get back."

Sally pushed aside any negative thoughts swimming in her mind and concentrated all her efforts on clearing her desk. It worked, too. The next fifteen minutes were more productive than she'd anticipated, and she felt a huge relief when she screwed up her final brown envelope and aimed it at the bin.

It was then that something hit her: she had expected Lorne to have returned by then. She dashed out of her office and asked, "Where's Lorne? I know she was going down to check on Abagun, has she returned yet?"

"That's a thought, I don't think any of us realised she was missing, boss," Joanna said. "We've all been busy doing the extra research."

Sally didn't wait around to hear anything else. She barged through the swing door and straight into Mick Green's chest. "Oh crikey, I'm so sorry, sir. I was in a rush and didn't see you there."

He brushed himself down. "That much is evident. Where's the fire, Inspector?"

"I need to see if Lorne is all right. I sent her to have a word with a suspect we're holding, fifteen minutes ago, and she hasn't returned yet."

"Come on, I'll go with you, you can fill me in on where you're up to on the investigation as we walk."

"Really?"

"Yes. Do you have a problem with that?" the chief asked.

"No, it's just that I'm eager to get down there, and holding a conversation with you at the same time…"

"We're wasting time. I've got a better idea, why don't I ask the questions and you answer them?"

"Whatever, sir. Can we get a move on? I have a bad feeling in my gut about this situation." Sally sprinted down the flight of concrete stairs ahead of him.

The chief flung a few inane questions at her on the way, and she'd intentionally mumbled her response, hoping he'd take the hint and leave her alone. She called at the reception desk to speak with Pat.

"Is Lorne still in there with Abagun?"

"As far as I know, ma'am."

"Shit, thanks, Pat."

"Is something wrong?" he called after her.

"I don't know," she shouted over her shoulder.

"She'll be fine, you're worrying unnecessarily," the chief said. He was trying hard to keep up with her, but his heavy breathing was an indication of how unfit he was, sitting behind his desk day in, day out. "Slow down, that's an order."

Sally came to an abrupt stop and spun around to face him. "With respect, sir. I've already told you I don't have the time to fill you in on what's been happening with the case. You're going to need to trust me, for now."

He caught up with her and placed his hands on his knees to catch his breath. Sally rolled her eyes. Luckily, he was oblivious to her rudeness.

"I do," he said. "What makes you think otherwise?"

"If you'll forgive me, I need to make sure my partner is safe, that's my biggest concern at this time." She continued on her journey down the corridor to the cell which had been allocated to Elijah. The door was ajar. Sally peered through the window and closed her eyes as relief flooded through her. Lorne was safe; she had one hand covering the suspect's clasped hands. He was in tears, and there was a box of tissues between them.

"Is she okay?" Sally almost jumped out of her skin when the chief asked the question behind her.

"Yes, she appears to be. I'll just check." Sally pulled open the door and stuck her head into the cell. "Is everything okay in here?"

Lorne smiled. "I believe so. Elijah had worked himself up into a bit of a state. I said I would stay with him until the panic died down."

"Ah, I see. And how are you now, Elijah?"

"Calmer, thanks to the kind lady. Please, do I have to sit in this cell… like a prisoner? I've done nothing wrong, not really."

"I'm sorry, you might think you've done nothing wrong, but in the eyes of the law, you have. I'm going to chase up the duty solicitor, see how long they're going to be. Hang in there. If you're truly innocent, then you have nothing to worry about."

"I am. Yes, I admit I got rid of the body, but I didn't kill that man, you have to believe me."

"We shouldn't keep you too long now." Sally jerked her head at Lorne, asking her to leave the suspect.

Lorne hugged Elijah and left the cell. "God, all this is wrong. That poor bloke is beside himself in there."

"Would someone mind telling me what the hell is going on around here?" Green demanded.

"Lorne, can you chase up the duty solicitor while I bring the chief up to date?"

"Of course." Lorne raced up the corridor ahead of them.

"I'm waiting, Parker."

Sally could tell by the tone he was using that the chief's patience had run out. "Sorry, would it be better to hold this conversation in your office, sir?"

"Maybe it would."

Sally's heart thumped rhythmically as he led the way down the corridor and back upstairs to his office.

Lyn Porter, the chief's secretary, glanced up as they entered her office. "Oh, hello, Inspector. I didn't know you were booked in for a meeting with the chief today."

"She wasn't," the chief snapped, answering for Sally. "We bumped into each other in the hallway. Can you get us a coffee each, please, Lyn?"

"I'll bring them in once the coffee has filtered. Nice to see you, Inspector."

Sally grimaced behind the chief's back once he'd entered his inner sanctum, and his secretary sniggered.

"Get in here, Inspector. Now."

Sally trotted after him and closed the door behind her. "Have I done something wrong, sir?"

"Take a seat and stop treating me like the idiot you believe me to be."

Sally sank into the chair and clasped her hands together in her lap until the whites of her knuckles showed. "I wouldn't dream of calling you an idiot, sir. I don't understand why you're so angry with me."

He sighed and glanced out of the window, inhaled a breath, and then turned his attention back to her once more. "I thought we had a long-standing arrangement that you would keep me informed about the cases you handle."

"That's right. To be honest, sir, my feet haven't touched the ground this week."

"Exactly why you should have involved me from the outset."

Sally slapped her wrist. "I'm sorry, I know I should have, but this week has been full-on, and at times I've not been able to breathe."

"Excuses, excuses. Now, tell me why Lorne has just hugged a suspect, in the cell downstairs."

"I'd better tell you the story from the beginning."

"Sounds like a good idea to me."

After Sally had filled the chief in, he sat there shaking his head and tutting at her. "You should have run this past me as soon as Pratt was picked up. I hope you and your team are taking this investigation seriously, Sally?"

Taken aback, she asked, "What makes you think that, sir? We've been at it all week. So far, we've discovered who the victim is and how he came to be dumped in the woods. On top of that, we've also arrested the two suspects who disposed of the body. I'm at a loss as to why you should believe we're not taking this case seriously."

"Because of what I've just witnessed downstairs, with Sergeant Warner. Should she be hugging suspects like that?"

"It doesn't hurt to show a little compassion in the line of

duty, sir, or are you saying that you're expecting me to reprimand Lorne for treating the suspect kindly?"

"There you go, twisting my words again."

"I'm not. All I'm trying to do is get at where you're coming from."

"Never mind. Have you questioned that man yet?"

"No, I've already told you that we're waiting for the duty solicitor to show up. He was panic-stricken, that's why my experienced partner was comforting him."

"I'm fully aware of the depth of Warner's experience, there's no need for you to point it out to me at every opportunity. There's nothing more for me to say except to offer you a word of caution."

"Caution, sir?"

"Not to get duped by the suspect. It all seemed far too cosy to me downstairs. These people are suspects for a reason, they got rid of a body rather than contacting the police."

"You're right. Is that all, sir?" Sally could sense her frustration building and was eager to get out of the chief's office before she really told him what she thought about him and his archaic ways.

"Yes, yes, I suppose you're keen to get back to it. Don't forget to keep me informed about the progress on this case. Will you drop by this evening, before you head home, to let me know how the interview went?"

"If that's what you want, sir." Sally gave him a half-smile, left her seat and made her way to the door, hoping he wouldn't say anything further that might tip her over the edge.

"I do. I'll see you later. Good luck with the interview. My advice would be, for what it's worth, not to be too soft on the suspect. He could turn out to be the killer you're looking for, despite him telling you that he's innocent."

"Don't worry, I'm an old hand at getting the information out of suspects, I've been doing it for nearly twenty years now." She didn't give him a chance to answer and swiftly closed the door behind her after she scooted out of his office.

"Get a telling off, did you?" Lyn asked, concerned.

"I think so. It's always hard to tell with the chief."

Lyn grinned. "No truer words have ever been spoken."

Sally waved and left the office feeling as though the chief was watching her under a microscope, and she detested it.

CHAPTER 7

Taking the chief's advice on board, Sally was tougher on Elijah than she'd intended to be during the interview. So much so that the duty solicitor, Mr Godey, had to warn her about her conduct.

"I want to lay my cards on the table," Sally stated. "I think we all agree that you and Pratt moving the body, or should I say dumping it in the woods, was a very foolish thing to do. I'm sorry, but if I let crimes like that go unpunished and word got out about it through the press… well, we can only imagine where that would lead, can't we? What I'm trying to say is, that the more you open up to us the more inclined we'll be to believe you when you tell us there was no malice intended in your actions and it was a genuine mistake on your part, even though I'm struggling to get my head around how getting rid of a body can be considered a 'genuine mistake'."

Elijah rubbed at his sore eyes. "I don't know what else I can tell you. I didn't kill that man, I didn't even know him, and yet, here I am, being arrested for a crime I didn't commit."

"Not exactly. You've been arrested for the crime you *admitted* committing; disposing of a dead body."

His gaze lowered to the table, and his shoulders shook.

"You can see how upset my client is. I suggest we call a halt to this interview for now, if that's okay with you, Inspector?"

"It isn't, not really. All we'd be doing is delaying the inevitable and, if you hadn't kept us waiting for two and a half hours, this interview would have been over long ago."

Mr Godey slammed his A4 pad on the table along with his pen and stared at her. "So, what you're effectively telling me is, the reason you're coming down heavily on my client, is because of what you regard as my tardiness, is that it?"

"Not at all, but if the cap fits."

Lorne's knee crashed against hers under the desk, a warning that she'd gone too far.

"Sorry, I should take that back. As you'll probably appreciate, I'm under pressure to get this crime solved quickly, not only for our sake but for the victim's parents' sake, too. They're desperate to lay their son to rest, just like any parent would be. So why don't we try and speed up the process here? Elijah, I want you to tell me how you knew to look in the cellar in your search for the source of the smell."

Elijah's hands swept over his face and through his short, tight, curly afro hair. "It was logical, that's all. I had checked the house thoroughly before Dick got there. He told me that, in his expert experience, the smell had nothing to do with the drains. Either I mentioned, or he spotted, the padlock on the cellar door. I'm so confused, I can't remember who said what now. The outcome is still the same. Dick went out to his van to fetch his tools. We had to gain access to the cellar. The smell was terrible, you must have smelt the corpse when you found it, it was vile. I could no longer live with the smell, it was rank, is that what you say?"

Sally nodded. "Okay, you gained access to the cellar and discovered the body. What happened next?"

"Dick tried to persuade me to call the police, but I got scared about doing that."

"Why, Elijah?"

He rapidly inhaled and exhaled a few breaths. "Because I'm from a different country, and the police there… they treat people appallingly."

"Are you in the UK illegally?"

"No, I swear all my papers are correct. I came here through the proper route, not via a dinghy across the English Channel. That's not why I was scared."

"Didn't Mr Pratt try to tell you that the police work differently in this country?"

"I don't know. He might have done. I was too worked up to listen to him. I pleaded with Dick to help me get rid of the body because I knew I would be the one who would get into trouble for it being found in the cellar. All I could think about was being deported, even though I hadn't done anything wrong."

"I can understand you thinking that way, but you still shouldn't have done it," Sally persisted.

"I believe Elijah is fully aware of that by now, Inspector, don't you?" Godey interjected. "He's also apologised numerous times regarding the issue. I think it's time we moved on."

"If you insist. Elijah, what can you tell us about your landlord?"

"I don't really know him. I rent the property from an agency. I pay them by direct debit every month. I've only dealt with the landlord a few times, and they weren't pleasant encounters, that's the truth."

"Which agency?"

"I'm so tired I can't think. If you give me my phone, I can access my bank account, that will give me the answer."

"I'll fetch it," Lorne was quick to volunteer and left the room before Sally could either agree or stop her.

They waited in silence until Lorne returned with the phone which she handed to Elijah.

He switched on his phone to access his bank account and shared the details with Sally. "There, it's Crown Letting Services."

"Thanks. We'll get in touch with them." Sally took the phone and handed it to Lorne who slipped it back into the evidence bag and returned to her seat. "Is there anything you can tell us about the previous tenants?"

"No, nothing. You'll have to speak to the agency. All I did was contact them about the property, went to visit it and agreed to the rental agreement."

"How long have you lived there?"

"Nearly six months. I love it, too. It is handy for work and situated in a nice neighbourhood. I've never experienced any racial abuse in the area, so always feel safe… or I did, until now. I was sitting in my cell, going out of my mind with worry. What if the killer comes back and murders me? It's all over the news now, isn't it? If the press learn that I've been arrested for getting rid of the body, the person who did this is sure to see the news bulletins and come after me."

"I'm sure it won't come to that. When we release you, and we will at some point today, is there anywhere you can go? Could you possibly stay with a friend or a work colleague?"

"No, I can't think of anyone. If I hadn't involved Dick in this mess, I could have probably stayed with him and his wife."

"How long have you known, Dick?"

"We met in the local pub, not long after I moved in. He was kind to me and offered me some advice about an issue I had with some fence panels in the garden. I tried to fix the problem, but I didn't have the tools. I asked him to come and take a look for me. He mended the fence and refused to take any money from me. So I bought him a few rounds at the pub. After that, we became solid friends. I've also recommended him to my colleagues, and a few of them have employed him to carry out several jobs for them."

"It's great that you've found a friend as good as Dick."

"I bet he's regretting knowing me now, after helping me out. Please, he shouldn't be blamed for what he did with me. In that respect, we're both innocent parties."

"At the risk of repeating myself, we can't have people going around dumping bodies and not taking the appropriate action against them."

Elijah held his hands up. "I'm guilty of that, what more can I say? But please, don't punish my friend, he was only trying to be kind to me, he's that sort of man."

"I'll see what I can do. I can have a word with the Crown Prosecution Service, and ask them to be lenient with you both."

He placed his palms together. "I pray that you can do that for us. I'm a good man, we both are… it's just that we panicked, and all common sense went out of the window. Please, please, you must believe me."

"I do, all I have to do now is make the people who have the task of determining your fate believe you as well. In the meantime, I'm going to ask you to be patient with us and sit in your cell."

He nodded and lowered his hands. "I'm happy to do that now that I've convinced you. I think this is the safest place for me to be until you have caught the killer."

Sally smiled. "I agree. I want to thank you for being honest with us."

"I'm a decent person, Inspector."

Sally ended the recording, and the constable standing at the back of the room stepped forward and asked Elijah to accompany him back to the cell. Elijah thanked his solicitor over and over until he left the room. Sally and Lorne escorted Mr Godey back to the reception area.

He gave Sally his card. "Can you call me later, and tell me how the land lies with the CPS?"

"I'll do that. Thanks for attending. Sorry for coming across as a miserable git during the interview. In my defence, I'd just come from a meeting with my boss, and he'd given me some poor advice on how I should treat Elijah."

"Tell me, Inspector, do you always listen to your boss?"

Sally and Lorne glanced at each other and laughed.

"Actually, we rarely do."

"Let that be a lesson to you then." He smiled. "I'll speak to you later. I'm sorry there was a delay in me getting here, that probably added to the tension."

"It's forgotten about now."

Godey waved and left the building.

Sally sucked in a breath. "I'm glad that's over with. And before you say anything, I know I was a bitch in there."

"At the end of the day, we're all under pressure to get this case solved. The chief was wrong coming down heavily on you and, in turn, you were out of order taking it out on Elijah."

"What would you have done in my position?"

"Back in the day, I would have told the chief to stick his job where the sun doesn't shine." Lorne peered over her shoulder. "Maybe I should have checked he wasn't standing behind me before I opened my big mouth."

"Nutter. Come on, we have lots to tackle before the end of the day. You go ahead. I think it's only right I should bring Pat up to date with what's going on with Elijah."

"I'll have a coffee waiting for you."

. . .

An hour later, Sally had been in contact with the manager at the agency who had agreed, as the property was still being regarded as a crime scene, to give her a list of the previous tenants as well as the landlord's name and address.

"Right, let's drop everything else and concentrate on the new information we have to hand, specifically the landlord, Neil Collingwood, see what we can find out through social media," Sally instructed the team. "Lorne, can you oversee things out here? I'm going to see what CPS have to say about the Abagun and Pratt situation."

"Leave it with me. Umm… can I make another suggestion, not wishing to step on your toes, of course?"

Sally rolled her eyes and nodded. "You know you can always speak freely, go on."

"It might be worth checking if Collingwood has a record, and I could ring the lab, and see if there was any other evidence or fingerprints found on Jessop's body that might lead us back to Collingwood."

"Now that, partner, is an excellent idea. Let me know how you get on."

Sally made herself another coffee and entered her office. She sat, picked up her phone ready to make the call to the CPS, but something else crossed her mind that she felt needed her immediate attention. She dialled Simon's number instead.

"Hey, it's me, can you talk?"

"Last time I looked I could. Why?"

"Funny, my sides are splitting."

"There's no need to go OTT. What can I do for you, dear wifey?"

"Likewise, there's no need to go OTT, husband dearest.

Seriously, can you talk? It's important to the case we're working on."

"Of course."

"Some information has come our way today, and I wanted to run it past you."

"I'm still listening." Simon groaned.

"All right, you impatient sod. What if I mentioned the name Neil Collingwood to you?"

"Hang on, Tony is sitting alongside me, all right if I put the phone on speaker? We're in the car, so no one can overhear us."

"Go for it. Hi, Tony, I hope he's behaving himself today?"

"Hi, Sal. Pass, ask me another."

"All right, you asked for it. Do either of you recognise the name Neil Collingwood?"

"It rings a bell. Might take me a few minutes to come up with a face to the name. Why? What's he done?" Tony asked.

"I think you're both probably aware of the investigation we are running at present. The body dumped in the woods?"

Both men said yes.

"Well, it turns out that the tenant found the body in the cellar of the house he is renting, and the door to the cellar had a padlock on it which only the landlord had access to."

"And the landlord is this Neil Collingwood, right?" Tony asked.

"Correct. He's also a property developer in the area, which is why I was keen to run his name past you guys. Have your paths crossed in recent months?"

"Hard to say. I've already told you his name rings a bell. Let me Google him, and see if a photo comes up," Tony replied. "Ah, yes. We've seen him at the auctions. We've not had a lot to do with him, though. I seem to remember we were bidding against him for a property only last week."

"That's great news, Tony, thanks. I don't suppose you can tell me what your impressions were of him?"

"If you're asking what type of character he is, I'd say he'd be well at home working alongside our troublesome nemesis, Granger. I noticed he gave us the evil eye once the gavel came down on the lot for which we outbid him. Not that he had the guts to say anything to us as we passed him in the foyer on our way to have a chat with the auctioneer."

"Hmm..." Sally said. "That's a name I never thought we'd hear again, not so soon after putting him in prison. We'll do some extra digging on Collingwood, see if we can find a connection between him and Granger."

"Glad to be of service," Tony said.

"You've been extremely helpful. Enjoy the rest of your day. Umm... I have to ask, why are you sitting in your car at three in the afternoon?"

"If you must know, we haven't stopped all day. We're having a quick bite to eat before we get back to it again."

"Is Dex with you?" Sally asked.

"No, I decided to drop him off at your mum's this morning, she was happy to have him. We weren't sure how our day would pan out, and it's quite warm today. I didn't want him to get overheated in the car."

"Thanks for always putting him first, Simon, I appreciate it."

"Hey, he's as much my dog as he is yours."

"He is. See you later, and I haven't forgotten that treat you said you'd knock up for me for tonight's dinner."

"Neither have I, it's all in hand."

"Love you both." Her attention was caught by Lorne appearing in the doorway. "Lorne sends her love, too."

"Sending it back to both of you, now bugger off and let us finish our lunch in peace."

Sally laughed and ended the call.

"What's going on?" Lorne asked and lowered herself into the seat opposite.

"I had an idea I needed to chase up before I rang the CPS and it involved Tony and Simon."

"Intriguing, tell me more."

"I wondered if they'd had any dealings with Neil Collingwood. Tony said he recognised the name and looked the bloke up on Google to view his photo. He said they'd outbid him on a property last week. He seemed a bit peeved by it, but nothing came of it. Then Tony mentioned that he'd put Collingwood down as a similar character to Granger, and that set the alarm bells ringing."

"I can see why. Shit, Granger was dodgy as hell. Want me to do some more digging, see if they've got any other connections?"

"In a minute. What have you managed to find out?"

"Joanna has been working hard on the list of previous tenants. I've located a few of them through Facebook. A couple of them have the workplaces listed, should we need to follow up on them."

"I think we should put that on hold for now and concentrate all our efforts on Collingwood. Let me get the ball rolling with the CPS, and we'll take another look at what our next plan of action should be."

Lorne agreed and left the room.

Sally rang her contact at the CPS, or tried to, only to be told that Melissa was on maternity leave for the next six months. So, she got passed over to one of her colleagues, Zoe Briggs. Sally explained the position to the woman, and Zoe promised to have a word with her boss as to how they would proceed, but she assured Sally that both suspects would be treated fairly, given the circumstances.

She ended the call and let out a relieved sigh then joined the rest of the team. Sally noticed the time on the wall clock as she entered the outer office; it was almost four-thirty. "Right, we're getting close to the end of play. Let's refresh what we have, folks."

Joanna started by recapping the research she'd carried out. "We've got four previous tenants we can investigate."

"Lorne and I have decided to set aside that information for now and concentrate on the landlord, Neil Collingwood. I think we should drive out to Acle first thing in the morning, surprise him before he sets off to start his day."

"I agree. Just the two of us, or should we take Jordan and Stuart with us?"

Sally chewed on her lip and contemplated the idea. "Why don't we all meet up at eight-forty-five? How do you feel about an earlyish start in the morning, fellas?"

"I'm up for it," Jordan was the first to respond quickly, followed by Stuart who chipped in with his agreement.

"Brilliant, okay, so let's get cracking and see what we can find out about the man before we leave for the evening."

Lorne raised her hand. "I think I've pretty much got everything we need."

Sally crossed the room to check the notes her partner had jotted down.

"He's definitely friends with Granger; might be worth considering us making a visit to see him, if things turn sour tomorrow morning."

Lorne grimaced. "If we have to, although I'd rather steer clear of that bastard if possible, bearing in mind what he did to Simon and Tony."

"I know he's an arsehole, but we should be used to dealing with dickheads like him. We'll park the notion aside for now, and I promise to revisit it if the frustration sets in. What about Jessop? Did Collingwood have any dealings with him on Facebook or the other platforms?"

"Not much from what I can tell, although he did make a few comments on Collingwood's posts now and again."

"So, that might be the link we need and one that we can reference, if Collingwood denies knowing the victim."

"Exactly. I've also established he's married and has a thirteen-year-old daughter."

"His wife's name?"

"Gina Collingwood. The daughter goes to a private school in Suffolk; it was pretty easy to track down the uniform she was wearing in a family photo he posted when she broke up at the end of last summer."

"Any other family members we should be aware of?"

Lorne shook her head. "Not from what I can tell. He appears to be quite popular, he's got over five hundred friends on Facebook. Lots of praise for the renovations he's completed over the years. I'd say his work is on a par with our husbands'."

"That good, eh?" Sally chuckled. "Does he live the high life? Exotic holidays, flash cars et cetera?"

"Apart from sending his daughter to a private school, there's not really much evidence of him throwing his cash around. There's the odd holiday here and there, but I wouldn't class them as expensive getaways, not that I'm an expert on the subject. Can't remember the last time I looked at a plane, let alone set foot on one."

"I know that feeling. Okay, let's call time on our day now and head home. Joanna, in the morning, you come in at your usual time and the rest of us will meet up…" Sally consulted the map around the Acle area and chose a location around the corner from Collingwood's house. "Here, in the pub's car park. How does that sound to you, guys?"

Jordan and Stuart both nodded.

"We'll make our own arrangements, meet up beforehand so we arrive in one car instead of two."

"Excellent. Rest up this evening, folks. Something is telling me we're going to have a long day ahead of us tomorrow."

SALLY DROPPED Lorne off at her house and arranged to pick her up at eight-fifteen because it was going to take them at least twenty-five minutes to get to Collingwood's house.

"Hey, how did your day go?" Simon asked. He left the pot he was stirring and wrapped his arms around her.

Dex jumped up and joined in the hug, too, which made everything all right in her world.

"This is nice and just what I needed; it's been a tough day. Do I have time to take the boy for a walk? I need to clear my head a bit before we sit down for dinner."

"I took him out earlier but I'm sure he'll be up for spending some quality time with his mum. Are you okay?"

"I'm fine. I could do with running through a few ideas. I know I should leave work alone once I get home, but we're planning on picking up the landlord of the property in the morning, and I want to ensure I've dotted all the I's before we embark on our mission."

"Sounds very cloak and dagger. Dinner will be at least half an hour. Will that give you enough time to mull things over?"

She lifted her head and kissed him. "It should do. I won't bother changing, I'll just slip on my trainers."

Dex understood what was going on and trotted out of the kitchen. She found him sitting by the coatrack, eyeing up his lead. She patted him on the head and removed the leash from the hook then swapped her ankle boots for her trainers, aware that she'd made that mistake once too often, taking Dex for a walk in her boots and ending up with a large blister under her big toe, so lesson learnt. "Come on, sweetheart, let's go clear our heads, well, mine at least."

They wound up at their favourite spot down by the river. Sally removed Dex's lead. He barked and bounced on the spot, eager for her to throw either a stone or a stick into the water, which was reasonably low after the dry spell they'd had recently. The summer had been hit and miss right across the country in the last few months, a mixture of showers and blazing hot days sprinkled here and there, nothing compared to what she'd experienced as a child. Summers always used to be reliably hot, back in the day. Not that she liked it too hot. Maybe while on holiday, but not when she was chasing dangerous criminals.

Is that what I'll be doing tomorrow, with the rest of the team, or have we got this all wrong? Just because Collingwood owns the property and knew Jessop, it doesn't automatically make him a killer, does it?

Lost in thought, it took her a while to realise Dex had dropped his stick by her feet and was impatient to get back in the water again. "Sorry, boy. Here you go." She threw the ten-inch piece of wood into the river, and Dex followed, causing a big splash.

A lady with a cocker spaniel appeared up ahead of them. She let her dog off its lead, and it dived into the river to play with Dex.

"Sorry, do you mind?" the woman called out.

Sally waved, recognising her as Brenda who lived a few doors down from them. "Don't be silly, they always get on well together. I didn't realise it was you to begin with. I need to visit the opticians. My eyesight isn't the best at this range."

"I used to be the same. Just don't let them persuade you to try bifocals. I did, and it was the worst decision I've ever made. I kept tripping over things. Actually, I came down here with Lady one night and ended up facedown in the river."

Sally tried to suppress her laughter but let it out when Brenda laughed and snorted herself. "Ouch, I bet that was embarrassing."

"Somewhat. It happened further back down that way. The thing was, to my dismay, I hadn't noticed a young couple making out and, well… I'll leave you to fill in the rest."

Sally wiped the tears from her cheeks. "Oh God, thank you. I needed that after the day I've had."

"My pleasure, you can always depend on me to tell you a few stories of the mishaps I've had over the years. I swear I could write a book."

"Why not? People need a good laugh now and again, you'd probably make a fortune."

Brenda raised a finger. "Might not be a bad idea. My son is always telling me I have a way with words. Okay, most of them contain two words and the second one is usually off."

Sally laughed again. "I've missed our little chats. I haven't seen you around for ages. Has everything been all right?"

"Sadly not. I lost my mother to dementia a few months ago. It hit me more than I thought it would, once I'd arranged the funeral and given her a good send-off. We were really close, more like best friends than mother and daughter. Damn dementia, it sucked the bloody life out of her at the end. The heartbreaking thing was that she no longer recognised me as her daughter, only as a carer coming into her home every day to tend to her needs."

Sally placed her hand on her friend's arm. "I'm so sorry, Brenda. I wish they'd find a cure for that godawful disease soon. We'd never even heard about it until about thirty years ago, at least. Mind you, it's probably longer, and now everyone I seem to meet has been directly affected by it, in one way or another."

"You're right. My grandparents never suffered from it, in fact, no one else has ever had it in my family, so we're mystified how and why Mum got it. Truly, I wouldn't wish it on my worst enemy. One day Mum was reading her books and all was great in her life, and the next, *boom*, her life as she knew it was over. In the end, it was a blessed relief to see her go. It's the guilt I have trouble dealing with, though… but you don't want to hear about that."

Brenda wiped away a tear, and Sally took a step forward and opened her arms. She hugged her neighbour, and Brenda accepted the kindness and warmth of the gesture.

"I didn't mean to burden you, love."

"You haven't. It's true what they say, a problem shared. You've been through an horrendous ordeal over the last few months. Had I known, I would have offered to sit with your mum for a few hours to give you some respite."

They parted, and Brenda withdrew a tissue from the packet she produced from her pocket. "I don't know how some people cope, caring for a loved one twenty-four-seven. I know a lot of people show empathy for others, but they don't realise just how hard it is on the carers…" Tears emerged again. "Seeing their loved ones fade before their eyes, despite their best efforts. Life is so hard at times."

"It can be. I'm sorry you've had to deal with this on your own."

"I wasn't, not really. My son and his wife have been amazing, but I was Mum's main carer. How people cope on their own… well, it doesn't bear thinking about. They must be saints, that's all I can say."

"Absolutely. Are you all right, love?"

Brenda smiled and reassured her. "I'm fine. It still hits me, mostly when I'm least expecting it."

"Have you considered grief counselling?"

"I'm on the list. I won't get to see a professional for months. By that time, it'll be too late. Like everything the NHS has to offer, there's a long waiting list for treatment."

"What about going private?"

"I haven't got the funds for that. Don't worry about me. How are you doing? You're looking well, despite your dodgy eyesight."

They laughed. Both dogs joined them, soaking them with the excess water they shook from their coats.

"Get out of here, both of you, you're as bad as each other." Sally threw the stick again.

Lady was much faster than Dex and retrieved the stick then swam around in circles, teasing him with it. Dex barked a few times to complain then chased Lady upstream.

"Don't go too far, you two," Sally called after them.

"I sense you're avoiding my question. Is everything all right, Sally?"

"Sorry, yes, just distracted by the dogs who never seem to have a care in the world. They have it a darn sight easier than us, don't they?"

"You're not wrong. How's Simon? Enjoying his new role, is he? I couldn't believe it when he told me he was changing careers."

"Thankfully, he made the right move. I have to say, he's a different person entirely. There were days when he'd come home from work a really grumpy bugger. Far from it these days. He still works long hours, but his enjoyment for his new job speaks volumes."

"That's great news. Good to hear the transition was worth it. Have you got any plans for the evening?"

"I've come down here to work through a major idea I have on the table for work tomorrow."

"Sounds intriguing, real cloak-and-dagger stuff."

Sally looked left and right and peered over her shoulder. "It is. If I told you, I'd then have to kill you."

Brenda snorted again. "Umm… on that note, come on, Lady, it's time we were making a move."

"Hey, in all seriousness, you've got my number, if you fancy taking a trip out for lunch one day—it would need to be at the weekend; we could take the dogs with us—just give me a shout. It's at times like this you need to have your friends around you."

"You're such a sweetheart. Thanks, Sally. Take care of yourself and don't work too hard, you hear me? Life really is too short as it is."

"Ain't that the truth? Take care, I'll see you soon… once I've been to Specsavers and sorted out my dodgy eyesight."

"Make the appointment soon."

"I will. Dex, come on, boy. Your father will be wondering where we've got to."

They parted, and Sally eventually encouraged Dex out of the water. When they got home, Simon was at the front door, waiting for them.

"I was getting worried about you. I'm guessing you had trouble getting him out of the water?"

"Sort of. I'll tell you all about it over dinner. I'll just dry him off, if that's okay?"

"Go for it. I'll start dishing up the dinner."

"What's on the menu?"

"It's a surprise. Don't be too long. I'll get you a towel."

Sally dried Dex off and gave him a quick brush then joined Simon at the table in the kitchen. "Oops, I'd better wash my hands. It smells delicious."

"Steak with a peppercorn sauce, fondant potatoes, broccoli and spinach. I hope you like it."

"Silly question, I adore it when you cook for me. You know how much I hate cooking."

"I do. Now, tell me what happened down by the river."

He listened intently whilst chomping on his dinner and even encouraged her to stop talking now and again to enjoy her food.

"That's terrible. No one deserves to go out that way. I remember seeing Brenda out with her mother, blimey, it must have been a few years ago now, before the illness took hold. She was such a friendly, bubbly woman. Christ, I'm talking seriously here now, if ever I get it, I've always said that I would end my life."

Horrified at his revelation, she dropped her knife on the plate. "What? You can't do that. I would care for you."

He raised an eyebrow and took a sip from the wine he'd carefully selected from his collection. "I wouldn't put you through it and I wouldn't want to live in a vegetative state, either. It's the vilest and cruellest existence known to man."

"But that's why I married you, to care for you in your old age."

"You're an idiot. Promise me you'll abide by my wishes. This reminds me, that we should explore the idea of making our wills and set up a POA for the future. Neither of us is getting any younger."

"Christ, sod you, I'm thirty-eight, not fifty-eight."

"And I'm eleven years older than you. The time is right for me, so I'll have a word with my solicitor, and get them organised in the next few months."

Unexpected tears welled up in Sally's tired eyes. "I hate it when we discuss things like this."

"I don't recall the conversation ever coming up before. It's a necessary evil and something we need to carefully consider for both our futures, Sally, it would be foolish of us to neglect it. Not that I have anyone else I can leave the house and business to anyway. And, if we're talking frankly about this, you should have made a will years ago, being a serving police officer."

"Crap, I guess you're right. I'll have a word with Lorne tomorrow, if we get the chance." She then made him aware of what the team's plan was for the morning.

"Let's hope you manage to track him down, if there's a possibility he's the person who killed Jessop."

Sally shrugged. "All the clues are leading us to think he's the culprit but, you know as well as I do, that things can change on a sixpence."

He raised a glass to her. "Good luck, if anyone can find the killer, you can. That's why I love you so much, I have the full package sitting in front of me."

"I'm dying to hear what comes next," she replied, slightly apprehensive.

"Nothing derogatory, I promise. Brains as well as beauty, and I wouldn't have you any other way. I've never told you this before, but if you drop off to sleep before me at night, I sit up and stare at you, count my blessings for having you beside me on life's wondrous journey."

The tears that had been threatening to spill dripped onto her cheek. "Aww… you say the nicest things, you old softie."

"Go on, say it, I'm mellowing in my old age, aren't I?"

She raised her glass, and he touched the rim of his against hers. "I'll drink to that."

CHAPTER 8

*E*veryone was in place. Jordan and Stuart had arrived minutes behind Sally and Lorne. They jumped in the back of Sally's car and drove towards Collingwood's house that was a couple of minutes' drive away from their location.

Outside the property, which was a grand manor house, not too dissimilar to hers, Sally went over what she expected from her colleagues a final time. "Lorne and I will approach the house. You two remain by the gate, just in case he bolts out the back."

"Nice place," Jordan whistled.

"Costs a fortune to live around here. It's one of my mum's favourite locations," Stuart added.

"Enough chitchat, we should make our move. Let's hope he's not observing us from behind the curtains in the bedroom." Sally flung open her car door.

"I can't see any twitching going on," Lorne replied.

They crossed the street.

"Good, I'd prefer to catch him unaware."

The two men remained at the gate while Sally and Lorne

walked up the herringbone block path. There were shrubs in full bloom dotted around the beds on either side of them as they approached the front door. Sally rang the bell. It was opened quickly by a woman in her early forties wearing a silky robe.

"Yes. Can I help?"

Sally flashed her warrant card, and the woman took a step forward to read it. "Are you Gina Collingwood?"

"I am. Why?"

"We'd like a chat with your husband. Is he at home?"

"No, sorry, he's out. He left early this morning. What's this about?"

"His name has cropped up during an investigation we're working on. We just need to clarify a few things with him. Can you tell us where we'd be able to find him?"

"I really couldn't tell you, that man is a law unto himself most days."

"Perhaps you can tell us when he's likely to be back?"

"Nope, can't tell you that either. No two days are the same in his line of business."

"Which is?" Sally asked, despite knowing what career Collingwood had chosen.

"He's a property developer, amongst other... things."

Sally detected the woman had slipped up and was determined to get to the bottom of what she was hinting at. "Other things? Such as?"

"Err... I don't know. This, that and the other. You know what men are like when a good proposition is presented to them."

"Such as?" Sally repeated.

"I don't know, you'd have to ask him that. I get bored the second he starts telling me how his damn day went. I'm sure I'm not alone, I bet lots of wives switch off, just like men do when we start talking about the latest fashion or what holiday we're interested in booking."

Sally smiled, if only to try and keep the woman onside. "I fear you're right. Could you give him a call for us?"

"Er… why would I do that? Can't you ring him yourself?"

"I can but sometimes I don't get a good reception when I'm on the road."

"Our phone is down. Didn't you see the workmen up the road?"

"I can't say I noticed them. Not to worry. If I leave you my card, will you ask your husband to ring me? It's very important."

"I'll do that. He's an extremely busy man, so I wouldn't advise you sitting at your desk awaiting his call. Like most men, he prefers to keep a woman dangling."

Sally grinned, playing along with the game she sensed the woman was up to. "They're awful, aren't they? Okay, I'll leave this with you. If you can emphasise how important it is for him to get in touch with me ASAP, I'd appreciate it."

"Surely you can give me a hint as to what this is about?"

"I can't, it's more than I dare do, divulging confidential information with a complete stranger."

Gina groaned and flicked her wrist. "Whatever, like I give a shit."

Sally acted as though she was surprised by the woman's comment. In truth, she'd been expecting it from the beginning of their conversation. "Oh, I see. That comment was a tad uncalled for, wasn't it?"

"If you think so. Now why don't you all bugger off and let me get on with my day?"

"With pleasure. Thanks for speaking with me, sorry to have inconvenienced you."

"Yes, you have." She slammed the door in their faces.

It wasn't until they walked away that Lorne whispered, "There was someone in the lounge, I saw the curtain twitch."

"I could tell the bastard was in there. How stupid do they think we are? His frigging car is sat on the drive, for fuck's sake."

"What are you going to do?" Stuart asked.

"We're going to get back in the car, drive up the road and park out of sight, see how long it takes him to leave the premises. My guess is that he'll take off right away, but not until he sees us drive off. If they want to play games with us, bring it on, we'll outwit them any day of the week. Bastards."

They got back in the car, and Sally drove off. Up ahead she spotted a lane, which was more like a dirt track leading to a farmer's field. She reversed into it and kept the engine running. It wasn't long before Collingwood's Land Rover darted past them at high speed.

"Shit, I bet he's seen us." Sally put her foot down, and the car surged forward.

"Maybe he's just in a hurry to get to an appointment," Lorne suggested.

Sally cocked her eyebrow and said, "Buckle up, folks. I'm not going to give up chasing him until he comes to a halt." She glanced down at her dashboard and the half-empty gauge mocked her.

Lorne leaned over. "I hope you've got enough petrol to continue the chase."

"Time will tell. Let's get some positive vibes going, folks. Negativity eats away at you when you least expect it to. Does anyone know where this road leads to?"

"It will eventually lead to Norwich," Jordan replied.

"I hope we get the chance to catch up with him before we reach the city, otherwise I reckon he'll end up losing us."

Sally upped her speed and flashed her lights at Collingwood. He refused to pull over. If anything, he put his foot down harder and sped away from them.

"You're fully loaded, and he's got the extra horsepower to get away from us," Lorne chipped in.

"Tell me something I don't know." Sally squeezed her foot harder on the accelerator, but it didn't have the impact she was expecting. "Jesus, it's like being involved in a tortoise and a hare race. No guesses which one we are. Sorry for letting you down, guys, this is the max I'm likely to get out of her."

"You might want to consider using your blues and twos," Lorne said. "That way, we can at least arrest him for failing to stop when requested."

"I'm hoping to throw more than that at him. Okay, hit them now."

The siren sounded, but Collingwood failed to take any notice.

"He's driving like a guilty man," Jordan said from the back seat.

"You're not wrong. Bloody idiot, it's his life he's endangering, going at over eighty on this road."

"All the more reason for you not to get too close to him. He's being reckless, asking for bloody trouble. My bet is he'll come a cropper, rounding one of the sharp bends ahead of us," Lorne said.

"Should I be pushing him this hard? Or do you think I should pull back, give him the chance to breathe and take my opportunity to overtake him when I think it's safe enough?"

"I'd keep up with him for as long as you can, for now. I'll get the map up; it might be worth us calling for backup to join us."

"They could use a stinger up ahead," Stuart added. "That's bound to have the desired effect and slow the fucker down."

"That's something we should consider. Lorne, can you

call the station? Make Pat aware of the situation and ask him to get a patrol car ready a few miles up the road."

"Sorry to put a dampener on that idea, but by the time uniform arrive, we'll probably have reached Norwich," Lorne said.

Sally lashed out at the steering wheel. "Shit, shit, shit." Her gaze flicked between the mirrors. "At least the road is quiet, that's a blessing. What to do for the best?" No sooner had she said that than Collingwood put his foot down and blazed ahead of them. "Jesus, he must have hit a sports mode button or something similar. We're never going to catch him now."

Within seconds, Collingwood had screeched around the hairpin bend ahead of them and was out of sight. Sally kept up the chase for several more miles, but it proved to be a waste of time and effort and they didn't lay eyes on his vehicle again. Two patrol cars turned up, and after Sally had a word with them, they took up the chase. Feeling despondent, she drove back to drop Stuart and Jordan back at their car.

Sally twisted in her seat to speak to Lorne before they got on the road again. "Damn, I thought we had him for a second there, I should have known his type would have more tricks up his sleeve than Derren Brown. What would you do in my shoes?"

"Umm... once I'd calmed down a bit, I would return to his house and take another shot at the wife, nailing her to the wall about her deception. She blatantly lied to us. He was there all along; she can't be allowed to get away with that."

"What are you saying? That we should arrest her?"

Lorne shrugged and stared ahead of her. "It's a tough call, one I'm glad you have to make and not me, but I wouldn't necessarily arrest her, not yet. Maybe go all out and scare the crap out of her. What about putting her under surveillance for a while, in the hope that she might lead us to him? Trace her calls? Mind you, they'll more than likely be using burner phones."

Sally contemplated her partner's suggestions for a couple of minutes and then concluded that going back to the house, to upset the woman, might indeed work to their advantage. "Let's do this. He's a bloody killer, that much is obvious after he blew us out of the water like that. We're quite within our rights to question his wife. Maybe we should take her down the station, show them both that we mean business."

"Whatever you decide to do, I'll be right behind you."

THEY DROVE the short distance back to the manor house, and Sally rang the bell. It took Gina Collingwood longer than it should have to answer the door.

"What do you want?" she snarled, the second she laid eyes on them.

Sally pushed past her and gained access to the house. "A chat with you. This time you're going to tell us the truth. We can either do it here, in the comfort of your own home or, if you prefer, down at the station, the choice is yours. I know which option I would choose."

"What? You can't come bursting in here like this, uninvited. Get out of my house. Now."

"Or what? You'll call the police? And there we have it, I think you'll agree, the upper hand is firmly with us. I'm sure the words 'come in' were used when you opened the door to greet us. So, why don't we cut the crap and get down to business? Here or at the station?"

"For fuck's sake... here will do." She folded her arms and tapped her foot in the hallway. It was obvious she had no intention of inviting them to conduct their conversation in another room.

Again, Sally kept up the pressure and took the decision

out of Gina's hands. "I think we'll hold our interview in the lounge, thanks for the offer."

"I didn't. You have no right coming in here, nosing around my house. Treating me like shit. I won't have it. I'm going to call my solicitor."

"Feel free. Tell him to meet us down the station in ten minutes," Sally called her bluff and grinned.

Gina grumbled a few expletives and barged past them to enter the lounge. "And no, I won't be inviting you to sit down."

"But we're going to do it anyway." Sally insisted keeping up the pressure on the woman; she could see how rattled she was with them being in her home.

Lorne and Sally sat on the cream leather sofa, and Gina threw herself into the armchair a few feet away.

"What do you want from me?"

"The truth would be nice, but I somehow doubt if we're going to get it. We'll see how we go. If you're not willing to speak with us, we'll take you back to the station. It's surprising how obliging suspects can be in an interview room."

"Now wait just a minute! What the fuck are you talking about? Suspect? I'm not a suspect, so why are you coming in here treating me like one?"

"You and your husband are both suspects. All right, granted, at first, we only had your husband in mind for committing the crime, but after the prank you pulled earlier, well, now you have also successfully put yourself in the frame."

Gina's eyes narrowed, and she firmly shook her head. "I didn't do anything, not intentionally, you have to believe me."

Sally cocked an eyebrow. "Are you trying to tell us the deception you pulled earlier was an accident? Because years of experience in dealing with hardened criminals is telling me otherwise. Why don't we cut to the chase? Tell us where your husband is, and we'll walk out of here without asking you anything else. On the other hand, if you refuse to tell us, I can assure you our line of questioning is going to be far more intrusive than you bargained for."

"And there we have it, a blatant threat. That's all you coppers know, isn't it? How to scare people into making confessions."

Sally nudged Lorne, and they both stood.

"Okay, let's play it your way. Gina Collingwood, I'm arresting you for perverting the course of justice."

"No, you can't. I haven't done anything wrong." Tears formed in her bright blue eyes, and she nervously wrung her hands in her lap.

"Talk to us, drop the act and be open with us. If you play by our rules, all this could be over in a few minutes, however, if you persist in telling us you're an innocent party in your husband's crime, then your fate will lie in your own hands."

Gina scratched her neck and then ran a hand around her colourless features. "I don't know anything, I swear I don't."

"You're clearly lying, it's written all over your face. Why are you covering for him? He's driven off and left you to face the consequences. What type of man does that to his wife?"

"He hasn't. If you must know, it was his idea to take off, to trick you and lead you away from the house. He doesn't want me involved in this."

"Sorry, but from what you've just told us, you're involved up to your neck, and nothing you have told us so far is going to persuade us to the contrary. Where has your husband gone? It's in your best interests that you tell us."

"I don't know where he's going. He told me to stay here while he drew you away from the house."

"And then what? He would lose us and double back here, was that his intention?"

"Yes, I think so. I don't know, everything happened so quickly. Neither of us was expecting you to come knocking on our door this morning."

"Good, it's always better for the police to arrive unannounced. It keeps criminals, such as you and your husband, on their toes."

"Stop calling me that, I've done nothing wrong."

"Haven't you? That's not the impression you're giving us. Deception can be classed as intentional, especially if it leads to a murderer escaping from us. Now do you see where this is leading, Gina? We could arrest you for being his accomplice."

Her face wrinkled, and the tears fell. "No, you can't label me like that." Snot bubbled at her nostrils.

Sally searched the room for a box of tissues; there wasn't one. In the end, Lorne passed the woman a packet of tissues from her pocket.

Gina blew her nose and sobbed. "I don't know what you want from me."

"The truth would be helpful. Where is your husband heading?"

"I don't know. He rarely tells me anything."

"What about the deception this morning? Was that down to him or was it your idea?"

"No, not mine. He told me to tell you that he wasn't at home. I pointed out that his car was parked on the drive. He got angry and told me to play along or else…"

She sobbed, and Sally could tell her fear was genuine.

"So he threatened you? How often does that happen?"

"More often than I care to remember."

"Did you know that he'd killed a man?"

"No, not until recently."

"When did he tell you?"

"After the name of the victim broke in the news. We

watched your conference together. He seemed a bit anxious, fidgety, wanted me to turn the TV over, but I was interested in what you had to say. It wasn't until a few days later when it came out who the victim was that he started really acting up. It was as if he knew it was him all along."

"Did he tell you why he was anxious?"

"He let it slip in his sleep, and I questioned him about it the next day. That was on Thursday."

"And did he tell you the truth?"

"Kind of. He told me that an accident happened a few years ago and it was now coming back to haunt him."

Sally nodded. "And you put two and two together."

"Yes. Then he told me he was putting the house on the market and we were moving abroad."

"And have you?" Sally asked before clarifying her question. "Put the house on the market?"

"Not yet. I have a group of cleaners coming in today, and the house stagers are coming in this evening. They think the house will look better for the photos with the lights on."

"Different," Sally replied. "Did he mention where he was hoping to move to?" One place came to mind, Spain. The Costa del Crime.

Gina avoided Sally's gaze when she gave her answer. "I don't think he's decided yet."

"Really? I think we can guess. What are his plans for the business?"

Gina shrugged. "Ask me something I can answer."

"How many properties is he developing at the moment?"

"I don't know. I keep out of his business."

"Are you on the payroll?"

"Yes, as a director."

"In that case, I find it hard to believe that you don't know much about the business."

"I know as much as he wants to tell me, which is the bare minimum."

"And you expect us to believe that you don't have a hand in the day-to-day running of it?"

"Believe what you like. He tells me I don't know what I'm doing half the time, so I can take a hint. I steer clear of it and tend to go out with my friends for lunch, a lot."

"And he's okay with that?"

"Yes, because it keeps me happy and out of his way at the same time."

"Where is he, Gina?"

"I don't know. He left not long after you called the first time."

"We saw him leave and followed him, but we lost him further up the road. I'm asking you to be honest with us and tell us where he is."

"I. Don't. Know," she emphasised every word.

"We're going to need a list of the properties your husband is in the process of renovating. Does he rent out properties as well?"

"A few."

"We're going to need that information, too."

"And where do you propose I get it from?" she asked, seemingly flummoxed.

"Does he have a home office?"

"He does, but I'm not allowed in there."

"For God's sake, how naïve are you? And you don't think there's anything suspicious in that, him keeping you out of the office?"

"No, it's what husbands do. My friends are always telling me they're banned from going in their husbands' offices as well."

Sally shook her head in disbelief and glanced at Lorne. "We need to get in there and have a look."

"I agree. Will you allow us to search his office?" Lorne asked.

"No. You're going to need a warrant. I don't give a shit about you coming in here, or should I say, forcing your way in here, but I refuse to let you nose around in his personal space. Anyway, it's permanently locked, and I don't have the key."

"We'll organise getting a warrant; okay, I've heard enough. I think you're holding back on us. Put your shoes on, you're coming with us."

"No, why? I can't, I won't come with you. I've told you everything you need to know."

Sally stared at her and said, "You have? If you don't allow us access to your husband's office immediately, then I must insist that you come to the station with us."

"Jesus, are you deaf? I said I don't have the key. It's padlocked."

"Hmm... your husband's preferred choice of preventing access to a room. We can make light work of that, if necessary. Where's the key?"

"I don't know, and that's the sodding truth. I think he keeps it on him. Bloody hell, I'm telling you the truth, and you still don't believe me, do you?"

Sally nudged Lorne and gestured to join her in the hallway. "What do you suggest? We get a warrant and take her in, or do you think she's given us everything she knows?"

"Hard to say. I think she's teetering on the edge of giving you access without the need for a warrant. We could call Stuart and Jordan, and ask them to join us. If they've made it back to the station, they can pick up some bolt cutters to make the job easier."

"Maybe we should ask for a warrant, just in case. Will you do that for me and then ring Stuart? Tell him and Jordan to get back here ASAP."

"Leave it with me. I'll be five minutes. Will you be all right in there with her, on your own?"

"Yes, don't worry about me. I'll use my spray if she starts getting antsy with me." She winked and patted her jacket pocket where she kept the permitted PAVA spray.

"Good for you."

Sally entered the lounge to find Gina had relocated and was staring out of the window. "Everything all right?"

"What do you think? How would you like the police invading your home?"

"I'd be fine with it because, unlike you, I've got nothing to hide."

She spun around quickly, almost losing her balance. "Neither have I. How many more times do I have to tell you that?"

"Why don't you take a seat? Can I get you a drink to help calm your nerves?"

"No, and you're not having one either, if that's what you were hinting at. I'd rather not have you in my home longer than necessary."

"I'm sorry you feel that way. Surely you can understand our reason for being here? We can't allow murderers to go free."

"It happened a while ago."

Sally frowned. "And you think that excuses your husband's part in the murder?"

"I didn't say that."

"You did, in a roundabout way."

"Here you go, typical police tactics of twisting my words to make me look bad."

"I didn't. Moving on. Can you tell me about your husband's setup?"

"Setup? What the fuck are you talking about? He's a property developer, and I've already told you that I don't know the ins and outs of the business. I know you're probably trying to catch me out, but think on, lady, I ain't falling for the oldest trick in the book."

"Maybe so, but it was a genuine question. Does your husband have a partner in the business?"

"Yes, me."

"You expressly told me that you were only a director. As far as I know, directors don't carry as much clout as a partner does, correct me if I'm wrong."

"I wouldn't dare. You think what you like, you clearly know everything there is to know about running a multi-million-pound business."

Sally smiled. "That much, eh? I'm not surprised he keeps his office locked if he's raking in that much. And how much of that is in cash?"

"Piss off. Don't be so ridiculous."

"Am I wrong in thinking that? Sorry, I just thought your husband might be the type not to like banks. Don't tell me there's not a safe in his office?"

"I wouldn't know. For the umpteenth time, I'm telling you, I never go in there and I don't know the ins and outs of the business."

Lorne entered the room and sat beside Sally. "All taken care of."

"Thanks."

"What is? What are you two up to? Christ, is it any wonder people in this country have lost all confidence in the police?"

"What makes you say that? Ah, yes, probably because the victim your husband killed two years ago has recently resurfaced, despite your husband's sinister actions to dispose of the body. Let's face it, this country wouldn't be in *the shit* it's in today, if we didn't have people like him roaming the streets. Funny how you're ignoring those vital facts about this investigation."

"You're hilarious, not." Gina turned the other way to look out of the window, not that she had the best of views from where she was sitting.

"So I've been told, numerous times before, usually when I've called someone's bluff. Go figure."

Gina remained silent and in the same position for the next few minutes. Sally bided her time, allowing the woman to go over her options in peace.

"I don't know what else you expect from me. I've told you everything I know but I don't think you believe me. So where do we go from here?"

"That's easy. We're waiting for two colleagues to join us. They're going to force open the padlock on your husband's office which, will hopefully give us the information we need to find him. Is it possible he might have travelled to Suffolk, to pick up your daughter from school?"

Gina turned to face them. "Why?"

"If he intends to flee the country, would he really leave her behind?"

"It was a passing fancy, said on a whim, that's all. I doubt if he would actually do it. You know what men are like, they're full of wise notions, but when it comes to the crunch, they haven't the balls to go through with their plans. My mum used to call him *one of life's dreamers*. She was right, more times than I care to mention."

"Maybe it'll be different this time, if he thinks his back is against the wall and we're on his tail."

She shrugged. "I can't answer that."

"What's your marriage like?"

Gina glared at Sally and fidgeted in her seat. "Why? What does that have to do with you?"

"It has everything to do with the investigation."

"I don't see how. Our marriage has been up and down for years, but we're still together because we give each other space. We're not in each other's pockets, unlike most married couples I know."

"Is he abusive towards you?"

After a moment's pause, she said, "Sometimes."

"If that's the case, may I ask why you're still with him?"

"No, that's none of your business."

"Because of the money? He supplies you enough to eat out all the time? Is that really enough to keep you satisfied, or does his generosity extend further than you frequently meeting up with your friends?" Sally's gaze drifted around the room. It contained items and furniture she would call plush, none of it likely to be found on the high street.

"He provides well for both of us, Chantelle and me. I have no complaints in that respect."

"Does he have any associates he works closely with? Or any family members who live close by?"

"The odd associate here and there. He's got a good crew working for him, that's how he's able to flip the houses quickly. And no, he's an only child, and his parents died years ago, his father because of a heart attack and his mother caught a bug while she was away. The parasite ended up eating away at her insides."

"Sorry to hear that."

"No, you're not. It was an absolutely terrible time for us. The doctors were baffled for months. By the time they realised what was wrong with her, the parasite had eaten half of her liver and one of her kidneys. She was in a sorry state come the end."

"How awful, I'm so sorry she and your family had to go through that," Sally said, in the hope that showing Gina some sympathy might make the woman warm to her, which in turn would possibly lead her to trust them.

"Thank you, you don't have to be kind to me."

The doorbell rang, and the moment was lost. Lorne left

the room to answer it. Gina strained her neck to see who it was.

"It'll be our colleagues, here to remove the padlock. This is your final chance to give us a key to the room."

Gina faced her and shrugged. "I would if I had one. I haven't, I swear."

Sally nodded and walked into the hallway to give Stuart and Jordan their instructions. They had come prepared for the task in hand; Jordan was carrying a pair of bolt cutters. Lorne followed the men upstairs, and Sally returned to the lounge to ensure Gina didn't make a run for it, like her husband.

Lorne came back downstairs a few minutes later to tell them the office was now open and that Jordan and Stuart were in the process of sifting through the paperwork to find what they needed.

Gina sobbed. "I feel violated. You coming in here like this, unnecessarily destroying my property."

"All this could have been avoided if you'd told us where the key was."

"I did, my husband has it with him."

Sally hitched up a shoulder. "Which is of no use to us, hence our need to gain access."

"I hope you're going to pay for the damage?" she shouted, her feistiness rearing its head again.

"You can put in a claim. Whether you'll be successful is another question that I don't have the answer to."

"Bloody brilliant, that is. You lot are useless. Utter tossers with a capital T."

Sally smiled. "You're not the first person to tell us that, and I doubt if you'll be the last. Do you want to reassess what you've told us so far?"

"No, why should I?"

"Because it will be easier on all fronts if you do."

"Screw you. I ain't saying nothing else. You standing there, giving me your fake sympathy. You think I hadn't cottoned on to what you were up to? Bloody idiots, the lot of you."

Sally smiled and left the room. There was a key in the lounge door. She locked Gina in and went upstairs. "How's it going up here?"

"Where's Gina?" Lorne countered quickly.

"I've locked her in the lounge. It might make her rethink the situation."

"I doubt it. She's one tough cookie. We've found a couple of interesting files, so we can make a start on those. He's got properties spanning the length and breadth of the county."

"Where do you think he's likely to hide out?"

"Maybe at a house that is already rented out but awaiting a new tenant."

"Have you found the name of the property agency he lets through?"

"We already know it; Elijah gave us that information. Crown Letting Services."

"Sorry, so he did. My mind is all over the place, wondering what he's going to get up to next. Can you call the agency, see if there are any properties that are empty?"

"I'll get on to them now."

Their conversation was interrupted by Gina banging on the lounge door, demanding to be let out because there was some kind of emergency.

Sally rolled her eyes. "I'd better see what she's making a fuss about, it'll be some kind of ruse, knowing what this family is like."

Lorne laughed. "Good luck."

Sally unlocked the door, and Gina wrenched it out of her hand.

"I have to get to the school; my daughter has had a bad accident."

Raising an eyebrow, not believing a word the woman was saying, Sally said, "That's not going to happen. Stop taking me for a fool, Gina. When are you going to realise that not all coppers are stupid?"

She shoved her mobile in Sally's face. "I'm not lying, see for yourself. The school rang me. You can't prevent me from going, I need to be there, ensure that my daughter gets the care she needs. You can't stop me, I won't allow you to."

Sally knew she was right, she couldn't stop her, but she could go with her. "I'll drive you."

"Shit! I don't want that. My daughter is unconscious. If she wakes up and finds you standing over her, she's going to freak out. Please, I promise I won't do a runner, this isn't a stupid ploy to get away from you. If you don't let me go alone, I'll be forced to get in touch with my solicitor. I'm not the one who has done anything wrong, my husband is."

Sally held up her hands. "Okay, stop getting yourself in a state. You can go. I want you to promise me that you'll contact me as soon as you know how your daughter is, once you get to the hospital."

"Of course I will. I can't thank you enough. My baby means the world to me. I need to pack a bag for her."

"I'll come with you, help you."

"I'm sure I can cope with packing an overnight bag for a teenager."

Sally nodded. Gina flew up the stairs, and Sally followed her but veered off towards the office at the top to tell the rest of the team what was going on.

"Bugger," Lorne said. She leaned in to ask, "Do you think she's telling the truth?"

"I saw the school's number listed as the last call she had received."

"Are you going with her?"

"No, she's asked me not to."

Lorne screwed her nose up and chewed on her lip. "Don't you think it's a touch convenient, her daughter having an accident the day her husband goes missing?"

"Possibly. Oh God, I don't know what to do for the best."

Gina appeared on the landing ahead of them. "All right if I get off now?"

"Are you going straight to the hospital or to the school?"

"I'm going to aim for the school, they told me there was a hold-up with the ambulance because of the strike taking place today." Tears welled up. "I hope that doesn't put my daughter's life in jeopardy."

"I'm sure she'll be fine. You go, keep in touch."

"I will. I can't thank you enough for believing me," Gina repeated. "I hope I make it there in time."

Sally was dying to ask what her daughter's injuries were, but she was conscious time was against them and didn't want to hold Gina up any longer than was necessary. "You get off. Drive carefully. We'll lock the front door when we're finished in here."

"Thanks." Gina raced back down the stairs, stopped in the hallway to slip on her ankle boots, collected a lightweight jacket and left the house.

Sally watched her reverse her Mercedes sports out of the drive. It wasn't until she sped out of sight that Sally paused to think about what had just happened. For some reason, her gut was telling her she'd been tricked.

Lorne took a step towards her. "Are you all right? You look as if you've seen a ghost. Sally, what is it?"

"Fuck, I think I've just made the biggest mistake of my career."

"What are you saying? That you think Gina was lying?"

"I need some space to make a call." She darted along the

landing to the main bedroom and saw all the drawers open. Gina hadn't packed a bag for her daughter at all, she'd packed one for her and her husband. Sally slammed her fists against her thighs. "Why, oh why, did I fall for it?" She withdrew her phone and looked up the number for the school. She rang and spoke to the receptionist. "Hi, I'm DI Sally Parker of the Norfolk Constabulary. I wonder if you can tell me if there has been any kind of emergency at the school today. Sorry, just to clarify, I'm talking about one pupil in particular."

"Not that I'm aware of. If you give me the pupil's name, I can check for you."

"It's Chantelle Collingwood."

"Just a moment, I'll put you on hold while I have a word with my colleagues."

"Thanks, if you could…" The music filtered down the line before she got a chance to finish her sentence.

It took a few minutes for the receptionist to get back to her. "Hi, sorry to keep you waiting. I wanted to be sure I was giving you the right information."

"And that is?"

"There have been no emergencies at the school today. I've also checked on Chantelle personally. She's attending her geography lesson. Is there anything else I can help you with?"

"Can you tell me if anyone from the school rang Chantelle's mother about ten minutes ago?"

"Hold the line."

Sally had to contend with another bout of crappy music.

"Hello, yes. My colleague received a call from Mrs Collingwood and got cut off, so she rang her back."

"What was the call about?"

"Mrs Collingwood wanted to know when she had to pay the final instalment for her daughter's trip to Italy next month."

"Great. You've been really helpful, thank you." Sally jabbed at the End Call button and screamed.

Lorne appeared in the doorway moments later. "What the fuck is going on?"

Sally covered her face with her hands. "Bloody hell, how could I have been so damn stupid?"

Lorne guided Sally to the bed. "Sit down and take a breath. What's wrong?"

"I fell for her lie, that's what. Jesus, how could I have been such a twat?"

"Stop it, Sal. It's not too late, we can catch her. We just need to come up with a plan." Lorne removed her phone from her pocket and rang the station, put the phone on speaker. "Joanna, it's Lorne. I need you to find out Gina Collingwood's registration number for her Mercedes sports and get it circulated right away."

"What? Of course. Is everything all right?"

"No, the woman has absconded. We need prompt action on this one, drop everything else, Joanna."

"On it now. I'll have a word with the desk sergeant, put an alert out."

"You're a star. Speak later." Lorne ended the call and then knelt on the floor in front of Sally. "Hey, mistakes happen, it's how we combat them that matters. Don't beat yourself up about this, hon. We have work to do."

Sally smiled at Lorne. "You're a good friend, the best. Thanks, partner."

"We've all been there, I promise you."

"I haven't, not in a long time. I screwed up when we investigated that case together years ago; apart from that I've been pretty solid ever since."

"There you go then. Look, Sal, we're only human. Come on, don't sit here in the doldrums, we've got work to do. A plan to devise."

Sally nodded and hugged Lorne who had to use the edge of the bed to assist her to get to her feet.

"Damn legs. Old age is creeping up fast."

"On both of us."

"Don't be so ridiculous. Come on, let's get a wriggle on."

They raced back to the office and filled Stuart and Jordan in on what had happened. Each of them gave Sally a sympathetic smile that she didn't need.

"What have you discovered? Wait, we should put a trace on both their phones, shouldn't we? Do you think he rang her while we were out of the room and they came up with the plan to deceive us, together? I should have taken a closer look at her recent calls list. I'm such a... feel free to fill in the appropriate name, if you dare."

"More than likely. Yes, putting a trace on their phones is a great idea. I'll ask Joanna to organise that for us."

"Thanks, Lorne." She stepped into the hallway to make the call and returned to the conversation a few seconds later. "All done. Joanna has had a word with Pat, he's raised the alert. If the Collingwoods are still on the road, it's only a matter of time before we find them."

"Let's hope so. We need to get on to the agency, and find out if any of his rental properties are empty."

"I'll give them a call," Jordan offered. He slipped out of the room and came back with the good news Sally had been hoping he'd have for them.

"A three-bed house over in Brundall. New tenants are due in at the end of the month."

"That's brilliant news. I think we should put this place under surveillance, just in case either of them tries to double back here, and then the four of us should shoot over to the address."

"Sounds like an excellent idea to me," Lorne confirmed with a wink.

CHAPTER 9

With the house secured and an unmarked police car with two uniformed officers positioned a few doors down from the Collingwoods' house, Sally and her team drove over to the rental property in Brundall. They surveyed the road. Lorne was the one who pointed out a Land Rover hidden behind a set of commercial bins on the opposite side of the road.

Seconds later, Jordan tapped Sally on the shoulder. "Over there, that's her sports car, isn't it?"

"It is. I have no intention of letting them get away again. I'm going to call for backup. We need to sit tight until the troops get here and hope they don't get wind of what we're up to."

They'd travelled to the location in two cars, and Jordan and Stuart had jumped in the back of Sally's car as soon as they had arrived. Sally lowered her window to get some fresh air and to clear the screen that had misted up.

"We could be in for a long wait," Lorne said.

"If that's what it takes to catch them. Has anyone got eyes on the front door?"

"I can see a glimpse of it. Would it be worth us taking a trip around the back, see if there is any extra parking available around there?" Jordan suggested.

"Yes, sounds good. I think we have to cover all the bases. Can you two have a look for me?"

Jordan and Stuart left the car and walked up the road to an alley at the side of one of the properties.

"Oh God, I hope this works and the couple don't have any more devious plans up their sleeves to punish us with."

Lorne patted Sally's thigh. "Forget what has happened in the past, it's the future that counts. Don't worry, we've got this covered. They won't get away from us again."

"How can you be so sure?"

Lorne held up her crossed fingers. "I have a secret weapon."

Sally creased up laughing. "You're nuts, you confirm it every day I work alongside you."

"Gee, thanks. Here they come now."

Their colleagues got in the back of the car again.

"The door was open, so I took the chance and had a nose around the inside," Stuart informed them. "There was no furniture in there, and the house was empty, didn't see them anywhere. When we came out, the neighbour asked us what we were up to. I showed my warrant card and asked him if he'd seen the Collingwoods. He told us he saw them drive off about half an hour ago."

"Fuck, how?"

"They had another car sitting on the drive."

"Sod it. I don't suppose the neighbour could give you the registration number?"

"Sadly not."

Lorne removed her phone and rang the station. "Joanna, you're going to have to give us a list of vehicles the Collingwoods have access to; they've escaped again."

"Oh heck. Leave it with me. I'll get back to you ASAP."

Sally covered her face and said the word 'fuck' several times.

"Hang in there. All is not lost," Lorne reassured her. Her mobile rang. "Hi, Joanna, you're on speaker, we're all here."

"Right, they have four cars between them. I've got a Nissan Qashqai and another Merc. I'll text you the registration numbers and I've already issued an alert for both vehicles at this end."

"Fantastic. Let us know if anything comes of it. We'll head back to the station," Sally took over the conversation.

"See you soon."

Lorne ended the call. "They're definitely craftier than any of us gave them credit for. Let's hope we find them soon."

"We should alert the ports and airports. Can you do that for me, Lorne?" Sally started the car and drew away from the kerb.

"Consider it done. There's no way they can get away from us."

"I hope you're right, partner." Sally considered what their next step should be while Lorne made the call to the relevant authorities.

"All actioned. We've cut off all available routes for them, if their intention was to leave the country."

"I hope you're right." Guilt trickled through Sally for letting Gina go. "See you back at the station, boys. Keep your eyes peeled en route."

"We will, don't worry, boss," Jordan said before he left the car.

Instead of starting the engine, Sally remained still as they watched Stuart and Jordan drive off.

"Are you okay?" Lorne asked, her tone full of concern.

"I will be, once the guilt dies down."

"You have nothing to feel guilty about, you hear me? Shit

happens, we're dealing with it. There's every chance we'll catch them."

"Will we? Between you and me, I'm choked up with the guilt."

"I don't know what else to say, sweetheart. You're wrong to blame yourself. Come on, you need to kick this guilt into touch. You've made a slip-up, that's all. It could have happened to anyone."

"But it didn't, it happened to *me*," Sally reminded her, jabbing a thumb at her chest. "Me, no one else."

Lorne released a never-ending sigh. "Enough, Sally. I can't sit here listening to this crap any longer. You're a fantastic copper but not when you're talking utter tosh like this. Can we get back to the station now? I think my caffeine levels are plummeting and I'm in desperate need of remedying the problem."

Sally tipped her head back and laughed. "In that case, I'd hate to be the cause of you going without the one thing that keeps you on an even keel. And thanks for the much-needed motivational kick up the jacksy."

Lorne's phone rang when they were about ten miles from the station. "Hey, Jordan, how's it going?"

"We've got eyes on the Merc. We're following it now, looks like they're heading towards Norwich."

"Where are you?"

"Just past Cringleford. There are two cars between us, so we don't think they've spotted us."

"Okay, we'll head over that way. Keep the line open, I'm going to put you on speaker."

Sally clenched her fist. "This could be it. Don't lose them, Jordan. Keep fully alert; too many mistakes have been made concerning them today."

"Don't worry, boss. We won't lose them, not intentionally."

Sally performed a U-turn on the main road. The driver of a Jaguar coming the other way blasted his horn. Sally knew there was enough room to carry out the manoeuvre without putting either of them at risk. She gave him a V-sign and flicked on the siren. The bloke passed her and saluted; she took the gesture as an apology.

"He changed his tune, didn't he?"

Lorne laughed. "Arsehole." Stuart and Jordan tittered at the end of the line. "How are things going there, Jordan?"

"We're holding back. The first car turned off at the previous junction, so we've decided to drop back a few metres."

"Keep us informed. We're five miles out from where you are and gaining fast. We'll kill the siren when we're a mile away." Fortunately, the road ahead was quiet, so Sally was able to keep her foot down. "Hold on tight." She reached eighty miles an hour within seconds. Out of the corner of her eye, she saw Lorne put her phone in her lap and cling to her seat with both hands. "Don't worry, I've got this."

"I bloody hope so, it's not only your life you're risking here, it's mine as well, and I'm not usually one for pointing out the obvious, but there's a sharp corner up ahead."

Sally laughed and eased her foot up to glide around the corner. "There, that was fine, wasn't it? You really should have more faith in my driving abilities."

"I have, I promise. Like I said earlier, I'm in dire need of caffeine to help keep me stable."

Sally laughed.

"Shit!" Jordan hissed.

Lorne picked up the phone again and asked, "What's going on?"

"The other car has turned off. We're going to drop our speed a little."

"Do what's necessary but stay with them. I'm switching off the siren now. We're about a mile behind you, we hope to be with you shortly."

"Good to hear, boss. The traffic is starting to build up more around here, just so you're aware."

"Got it." Sally eased down on the accelerator a tiny bit more, hoping that Lorne wouldn't notice.

"God, I hope we catch them this time. I'm not sure I'll be able to cope if they get away from us again."

"Ha, and there you were, trying to keep my spirits up back there." Sally turned and grinned.

"Do you have to do that? I'd rather you kept your focus on the road. I'd much prefer to catch up with them in one piece."

"We will, don't worry."

Another five minutes flew past.

"There, isn't that Stuart's car up ahead?"

"Yes, I can't believe we've managed to catch up with them."

"I told you that you should have more faith in my driving skills. Jordan, can you see us?"

"I can, boss. Do you want to overtake us?"

"I was about to suggest the same. I'm coming through, and if the opportunity arises, I'm going to overtake the Collingwoods as soon as I can, then we'll have them sandwiched between us."

"Excellent idea. There's no way they'll be able to escape us again."

"I hope not. Making my move now." Sally soared past Stuart and Jordan and tucked in behind the escapees.

"That was a neat move," Lorne praised.

Sally evaluated the traffic and the road ahead before she leapfrogged the Collingwoods. "Okay, we've got them where we want them now. The sign is telling me that Norwich is five miles up the road. I think we should make our move now."

"I agree," Jordan said. "Less chance of them veering off down a side street, being this far out."

"Exactly. Five, four, three, two, one." Sally slammed on the brakes. The car slid sideways, blocking the lane. "Prepare for impact, Lorne."

"Holy crap," Lorne shouted and closed her eyes.

However, in the end, the impact was averted. Sally shot out of the vehicle once the Mercedes came to a halt. Jordan and Stuart did the same, but Lorne remained in the car with the Collingwoods' bumper four inches from the passenger door.

The driver's door was shoved open, and Neil bolted through the hedge at the side of the road and across the nearby field. Anxiously, Sally watched Jordan and Stuart chase after him. They returned with Collingwood a few moments later, wriggling like a worm caught on a fishing line.

"Slap some handcuffs on him and get him back to the station, we'll deal with his wife."

Neil was marched away and placed in the back of Stuart's car.

"Get out of the vehicle, Gina. Don't try anything foolish."

The disgruntled woman opened her car door and shouted, "I haven't done anything wrong, he forced me to do it. Told me he'd take my daughter away from me if I didn't meet him."

Sally rolled her eyes, sensing the scheming woman was playing yet another game with them.

"We can thrash this out down at the station. Put your hands out."

Gina hesitated for an instant and then offered up her

wrists. Sally slapped the cuffs on and then steered her towards her car. Placing a hand over the woman's head, she assisted her into the back seat. The traffic was slowing down in the opposite lane, the drivers rubbernecking.

Sally bent down to check Lorne was okay. "Are you all right?"

"I've survived worse. What are you going to do about their car?"

"We'll get it picked up. I'll tuck it in, closer to the hedge, that way it won't be holding up the traffic."

Back at the station, Sally gave Jordan and Stuart five minutes to process Neil Collingwood before she and Lorne removed Gina from the car.

"Please, don't do this, I've done nothing wrong. I want my solicitor."

Sally clasped her cuffed hands and pulled her towards the entrance. "I sense your solicitor is going to be very busy over the next couple of hours. We'll interview your husband first, after we've made you comfortable in your cell."

The tears flowed, but Sally chose to ignore them.

"I can't go to prison. I didn't do anything wrong. Any decisions I made were under duress."

"Tell that to your solicitor, I've heard enough of your lies for one day."

The woman stared at her. Eyes blazing, she spat at Sally. Luckily, her aim was hopeless.

Sally glanced down at the blob of spit at her feet. "I see you're finally showing your true colours."

"You ain't seen nothing yet, bitch."

Sally grinned and yanked on the cuffs, forcing the woman down the hallway to the custody suite. "Here's another one for you, Frank. Make her comfortable, she'll be second on the interview list. I'll get to her in a few hours."

"Leave her with me, ma'am, she'll be in safe hands."

Sally winked at the custody sergeant and left the area with Gina shouting expletives behind her. She turned the corner to find Lorne waiting for her at the bottom of the stairs.

"Let's grab that coffee you keep going on about. We'll let Collingwood get accustomed to his cell for half an hour or so; that'll teach him for trying to escape. His solicitor can wait, too, when he finally shows up."

"No one messes with you, right?"

LORNE JOINED Sally in the office, and together they made notes for the interview. After receiving the call, informing them that the solicitor had arrived, they went downstairs and joined Collingwood and his solicitor in Interview Room One. Sally made the introductions and, with a young male officer standing at the back of the room, she started the recording.

"It's nice to finally meet up with you, Mr Collingwood. Is it all right if I call you Neil?"

"Whatever," he replied churlishly.

"Perhaps you'd like to explain why a body was found at one of your rental properties at the beginning of the week?"

"No idea, ask the tenant, there have been a few over the years."

"To our knowledge that's correct, but there's only one person who had a key to the cellar of that property, and that person would be you. Why did you kill Dan Jessop and hide his body in a freezer in the cellar?"

After having a whispered conversation with Mr Tyler, his solicitor, Neil replied, "No comment."

"Fair enough. I believe you've been poorly advised to go down the 'no comment' route, but that's your choice. The evidence, as they say, is stacking up against you. Your determination to avoid us today and to encourage your wife to meet up with you, probably to deliver your passport, speaks volumes about how guilty you are of the crimes you've committed."

"What crimes?"

"As already stated, the murder of Jessop, and don't worry, we'll be sending officers out to your other properties, searching for additional bodies you've possibly buried during the renovations you've carried out over the years."

"You can't do that. I won't allow it." He turned to face Mr Tyler. "Tell her, she can't do that."

Tyler raised an eyebrow and shrugged. "I think you'll find she's quite within her rights to do it, if a body has already been found at one of your properties."

"What the fuck? Whose side are you on? You told me not to fucking say anything, and here you are, spouting your fucking mouth off."

Sally smugly watched the exchange between the solicitor and his client. Once they'd finished bickering, she asked, "Why did you kill him?"

"I didn't."

"Come now, may I remind you that the CPS are likely to go easier on you if you admit killing Jessop."

"That's bullshit and you know it. You can't trick me like that."

Sally shrugged. "Why did you kill him? Did he outsmart you over a property?"

"No."

"Did he do the dirty on you?"

Collingwood stared at her and refused to answer.

"Why did you kill him and hide his body in the freezer?" she persisted.

"Because I could," he admitted.

His solicitor whispered something in his ear.

Collingwood slammed his fist on the table. "Shut up. When I want your opinion, I'll ask for it."

Sally raised a hand. "Can you calm down, Mr Collingwood? All this anger isn't getting you anywhere."

"It might not be, but it's making me feel better. I've had enough, I'm tired and hungry. You haven't fed me since you brought me in. I've been told the food ain't bad around here, prove it."

"You're not entitled to eat, not after only spending half an hour in your cell. Can we get back to the interview now?"

"Whatever. No comment, no comment, no comment. There, that's all you'll be getting out of me from now on. Got the message yet?"

"I have. So, I'm going to tell you how I believe things went down, the day you killed Dan Jessop."

He crossed his arms and glared at her. "This should be interesting. Shall we compare notes?"

"We know there was a connection between you and Jessop. You really should be careful who you friend or what you post on social media. I'll be checking in with his girlfriend later to see if you ever worked with Dan on a project or not."

"Good luck with that one, the bitch is a bare-faced liar, most women are."

"In your opinion."

"*My opinion* is the only one that matters."

Sally shrugged, deciding his comment wasn't worth a response. "Go on then, tell me how Jessop's body got to be in the freezer."

"You seem to have all the answers, you tell me."

"I believe your paths crossed, probably at an auction house. What happened, did he double-cross you? Perhaps he did a better job on a renovation than you and you were envious of his achievements and decided he needed to be taken out. How am I doing?"

"No comment."

"Ah, you've just proved that I must be close to the truth."

"Bollocks to that."

"How many more bodies are we likely to find at your properties?"

"No comment."

"Was your wife involved in the murder?"

"No comment."

"Was she involved? If you don't reveal the truth, we'll be charging her with being an accessory to the murder. She's already shown us today that she can't be trusted."

"She wasn't part of it. She knew nothing about the incident until the other day. So, you can sod off and keep her out of it."

Sally smiled, knowing he'd succeeded in putting yet another nail in his coffin with his unintentional slip of the tongue. "And your daughter? Does she know her father is a murderer?"

His eyes narrowed, and his lip curled. "Keep her out of it, as well."

"What do you think she's going to say when she finds out?"

"No comment. Keep both of them out of it, they know fuck all."

"And yet you have used both your wife and your daughter in your futile attempt to escape us today."

"No comment."

Sally slammed her notebook shut. "Then I have nothing

further to say to you for now. Time to see what your wife has to say about all of this, and then we'll bring your daughter in and ask her what she knows. Looks like we have a very busy day ahead of us, Sergeant."

"It does, boss," Lorne said, playing her part.

"I've warned you, I won't say it again, leave my family out of this."

"Ah, see, warnings coming from a murderer don't wash with me. Interview completed at four-thirty."

"We'll see about that, bitch. You ain't heard the last of this. Well, tell her, you frigging idiot, what the fuck am I paying you for?"

Mr Tyler closed his pad, tucked it into his briefcase and walked towards the door. "I'll be in touch soon, Mr Collingwood. In the meantime, I would suggest you behave yourself."

"Fuck off, you useless prick."

"I'll wait in the reception area. Call me when you intend to interview Gina," Mr Tyler said then left the room.

"Oh dear, falling out with your brief isn't ideal, is it?"

"Piss off, who asked you? People on my payroll do what I tell them to do, or they can fuck right off."

"Take him back to his cell," Sally ordered the uniformed officer.

He was led out of the room.

"That was tough. He kind of admitted, here and there, that he killed Jessop but didn't come right out and say it."

Lorne nodded. "He did. It's only a matter of time before he breaks. He gets his knickers in a twist too often not to. Do you want me to get Gina, or are you going to leave her for a while?"

"No, we might as well get it over with this afternoon."

Lorne darted out of the room and returned with Gina

Collingwood and Mr Tyler. A female officer joined them, taking up her position at the back of the room.

Gina had red eyes from where she'd been crying in her cell since they'd arrived.

Sally began the interview. "Gina, were you involved in the murder of Dan Jessop?"

"No, I was not," she replied adamantly, her voice shaking.

Sally noticed a significant change in her demeanour since she'd had the chance to cool off in her cell. "Why did you deceive us today and meet up with your husband?"

"He left me no choice, told me I had to join him, or I'd never see either him or my daughter again. He told me he had Chantelle with him; he lied. You have to believe me, he had me by the short and curlies. I didn't want my daughter to be a part of this."

"Has he abused you in the past?"

"Yes. That's why I decided to send my daughter away to school, so he couldn't take his anger out on her."

"Is he a volatile man?"

"Absolutely."

"What did you know about the murder he'd committed?"

"I didn't. It was a shock when he blurted it out this week after he saw the news bulletin about a body being found in the woods. It was as if he knew it would be Jessop, despite him storing it in a freezer. That confirmation came via the press a few days later. He bought a couple of newspapers every day, to check if the body had been identified and panicked when he discovered it had."

"That's when he started to make plans to leave the country, right?"

"Yes, but he didn't realise the amount of hassle involved in organising his escape plan. He gave me a list of jobs to do. I was working my way through them when you showed up at our front door. He was terrified of getting caught and ran out the back. He rang me, and told me he was going to keep his head down at one of his properties. He kept calling me every half an hour, to check what I was up to, then ordered me to trick you and go to him. He threatened to kill my daughter if I didn't do it."

"And where was he intending to flee to?"

"Spain. He's got some friends there, well, they're more associates really. There's more."

"I'm listening."

"He's been shifting drugs. I had no idea he was into dealing that shit until a few months ago. I told him I didn't want any part of it. That's when the abuse really started. I'd made a few threats that I was going to leave him; he feared losing me. I couldn't cope with being the cause of a mother losing her son or daughter because of him supplying them with that filth. He told me I didn't have a say in his business, never had and never would. I knew that day that my marriage was finished but I had to think carefully, put a plan in place before I told him I was leaving him. I can't apologise enough for the way I've reacted today, I was scared, knowing that he's already killed someone."

"Would you be prepared to stand up in court and tell a jury what you've just told us?"

"Yes, if it means putting him inside, so my daughter and I are out of harm's way."

"Thank you. I have a few more questions, then you'll be free to go."

"Free? You believe me?" The relief was evident in her features.

"Yes." Sally asked several extra questions about the couple's finances and then ended the interview. "You'll be asked to surrender your passport."

"I don't mind. As long as he's banged up. He will be, won't he?"

"You have my word."

Mr Tyler thanked them and escorted Gina out to his car after he'd offered to give her a lift home.

"I hope I've done the right thing, releasing her?"

"You have. I think she's innocent, just misguided. She was obviously looking out for her daughter, trying to protect her the best way she knew how, by going along with him."

EPILOGUE

The following day, Sally and Lorne interviewed Collingwood twice more, morning and afternoon, with several hours' break in between sessions. She could tell they were wearing him down because he opened up further each time they spoke with him.

At the end of a long day, Sally finally made the decision to charge him with the murder of Dan Jessop as well as absconding from the police during their enquiries.

That meant that Dick Pratt and Elijah Abagun were cleared of all charges. The CPS understood that the two men panicked when they'd discovered the body and now that they had the murderer in custody, the two men would have to serve a community service order. Sally had the pleasure of visiting Elijah to share the news. Relieved, the poor man broke down and cried.

"I'm so, so sorry. I promise I will be a law-abiding citizen from now on."

"I'm glad to hear it, and don't be so scared of the police in the future. We're not all bad. There are a few of us who are intent on doing the right thing for the people of this country."

"I know that now. Back in Nigeria… well, I'd rather not consider the punishment I would have received, even though I had nothing to do with that body being in my cellar."

Sally smiled. "You're safe here. I'll give you my card. If ever you're in trouble, don't hesitate to get in touch with me."

"Oh my, you really are too kind. I'm a good man."

"I can tell. Now go and live the best life you possibly can, Mr Abagun."

He took a step forward and hugged her.

Sally laughed and patted him on the back. "Can you let me go? I'm having trouble breathing."

"Oh no, I didn't mean to hurt you, I was only trying to show you my gratitude for believing in me."

"It's fine, and you're welcome."

He bowed, backed away and waved over his shoulder.

Sally returned to her team and applauded them. "You all played your part in solving this investigation. I'm so grateful to have every single one of you as part of this special team. I'd like to invite you and your partners to a barbecue at my place next Saturday after we've wrapped up all the paperwork for this case. What do you reckon, folks, are you up for it?"

Without hesitation, every member of the team nodded and smiled.

"We'd love to, boss," Jordan said, acting as spokesperson for the group. "Shall we bring anything with us?"

"Just yourselves. Lorne, can you join me in the office?"

Sally led the way. "Take a seat. Will you give me a hand with the paperwork on this one? I just want to ensure that I cross all the T's et cetera, bearing in mind the cockup I made, letting Gina go."

Lorne shook her head. "Of course I'll help you, but you're

doubting yourself when there's no reason to, Sally. Have you had a word with the chief yet?"

"I'm just about to head over there. I can't say I'm looking forward to it. I suppose our last conversation was a bit... strained."

"To break the ice, why don't you ask him to come to the barbecue? Or would you feel awkward inviting him to join us?"

"Gosh, I'd never even considered asking him. To be honest, I'm not sure how I'd feel about him being there, at the team's celebration dinner. It's not like he played a part in our success, is it?"

"No, but it would show him that you're not the type of person to hold a grudge."

* * *

SALLY CALLED out to Simon to bring another bottle of wine with him. He appeared beside her within seconds and opened the special red he'd raided from his collection.

"I'll do the honours. You're needed over there because your boss has just arrived."

"Oh heck, I was hoping he'd call and make an excuse not to be here this evening. Oh well, I'd better show willing." She pecked him on the cheek and crossed the patio to welcome DCI Green. "Hello, sir, I'm glad you were able to join us. No plus-one with you this evening?"

"Not this time. I might as well tell you, that my wife and I split up a couple of months ago. Apparently, I wasn't exciting enough for her."

"Ouch, that must have been hard to hear, sir, I'm sorry."

"I'm okay. I think we drifted apart years ago; it's called life. You have a lovely home, Inspector, sorry, Sally."

"Simon owned it long before I came on the scene."

"He's a good man. I've heard on the grapevine he's doing exceptionally well as a property developer, along with Lorne's husband. I hope you ladies aren't considering joining them in their successful venture?"

Sally winked. "I can't say I haven't been tempted after taking some flak from you in the last two or three months."

"What? Are you serious? If I've been out of order, I apologise. Maybe I've been guilty of letting my personal life occasionally affect my working day."

"We all have our burdens to bear at times. Maybe you'll be more understanding when I have a blip in the future."

Lorne hooked her arm through Sally's. "Not interrupting, am I?"

"No, DCI Green was just heaping praise on us for another job well done, weren't you, sir?"

"I was. I don't say this often enough, to either of you, but I'm extremely proud of what you've both accomplished since the Cold Case Team was formed."

Simon appeared with a tray of glasses. "Hey, I thought I made it perfectly clear that there was to be no shop talk tonight."

"You did, and we wouldn't dream of it. Now when will the food be ready? I'm starving, and the boss looks like he hasn't had a decent meal inside him for ages."

Green raised his glass to Sally. "A nice juicy steak would be gratefully received. I've heard great things about your husband's cooking."

"You won't be disappointed, sir. I'm glad you decided to join us. Here's to the future." Sally clinked her wine glass against his.

"Whatever that holds, for all of us."

THE END

. . .

THANK you for reading Frozen In Time. The next book in this exciting cold case series Echoes of Silence is now available.

IN THE MEANTIME, have you read any of my other fast-paced crime thrillers yet? Why not try the first book in the DI Sara Ramsey series No Right to Kill

OR GRAB the first book in the bestselling, award-winning, Justice series here, Cruel Justice.

OR THE FIRST book in the spin-off Justice Again series, Gone In Seconds.

WHY NOT TRY the first book in the DI Sam Cobbs series, set in the beautiful Lake District, To Die For.

PERHAPS YOU'D PREFER to try one of my other police procedural series, the DI Kayli Bright series which begins with The Missing Children.

OR MAYBE YOU'D enjoy the DI Sally Parker series set in Norfolk, Wrong Place.

. . .

Or my gritty police procedural starring DI Nelson set in Manchester, Torn Apart.

Or maybe you'd like to try one of my successful psychological thrillers She's Gone, I KNOW THE TRUTH or Shattered Lives.

KEEP IN TOUCH WITH M A COMLEY

Pick up a FREE novella by signing up for my newsletter today.
https://BookHip.com/WBRTGW

BookBub
www.bookbub.com/authors/m-a-comley

Blog

http://melcomley.blogspot.com

TikTok
https://www.tiktok.com/@melcomley

Why not join my special Facebook group to take part in monthly giveaways.

Readers' Group

Printed in Dunstable, United Kingdom